Dreaming about Love

The Coming of the Angels

Dreaming about Love

The Coming of the Angels

ROBERT SORIN BAICU

CRISTINA MARIA DONE
2019

Robert Sorin Baicu

Dreaming about Love-The Coming of the Angels-vol 2

2019

ISBN 978-0-359-56899-4

Distributed by Lulu.com

Published by Cristina Maria Done

Text and translation Cristina Maria Done

Cover Design Robert Sorin Baicu

A CIP record for this book is available from the Library of Congress Cataloging-in-Publication Data

Cristina Maria Done

Phone: +40 0729 291 014/
Email; donecristina80@gmail.com

Dedication

”To my wonderful, most beautiful fairy… ”

If it wasn’t you in my life, my dear Crissy, everything would be just…a simple love dream!

Robert Sorin Baicu

Acknowledgements

I would like to thank my wife and editor Cristina Maria Done, my friends Stefan Apostol and Magda Bacescu, without whose help this book would never have been completed.

Thank you for your patience and guidance.

Robert Sorin Baicu

Foreword

A drop of reality can create millions of fantastic universes ... At one point, they can become real if ...really believe they can exist.

Baicu Sorin-Robert

I did not think a love story would turn into a novel. Frankly, the love of Crissy and the man who made her immortal, Robby, broke me to pieces.

I wanted the love to become real and the two of them to meet. I did not get their dream idle. It was something beautiful, pure, mysterious, but incomplete.

I read and read and I wanted their love to be fulfilled, but ... the story ended and their worlds did not merge into the sea of love that springs from my soul.

Then I did not know that a drop of reality and hope can create millions of fantastic universes. I did not think that at some point these universes can become real if there is truly faith.

Perhaps the gap in Robby's soul had moved to me. Maybe Crissy's transformation affected me more than I thought it was possible.

It never happened to me, to identify myself so profoundly with a character of a story.

How many times have I read the first volume? I do not even know. I just know the first time I read in the subway. And?

The mechanic has awakened me from day dreaming. Ma'am, I got to the end of the line. Funny right?

Something in me hoped things would not stay that way. I wanted a sublime happy end.

When I found out that it was going to be the second volume, I screamed with joy. I started dancing around the house. The outcome? My neighbors knocked at the door, wondering what had happened.

Since then, waiting for the second volume seemed an eternaty. We did not eat any more, we did not sleep anymore, and during the day we were day dreaming. Why?

Had I gone mad? No!!!

I realized I was becoming Crissy and the writer was Robby.

Even if the details could not be revealed to me, I felt the two of them would meet.

How? When? Where? It did not matter anymore.

The feverishness of the writer, eager to render beautiful and complex paintings, contaminated me, and it seemed as if every character in the first volume came before me promising solemnly that he would be present in volume two. I also received new characters in the audience. Splendid! So, I was witnessing a true science-fiction masterpiece.

My universe was beautiful, love was sublime, everything was magnificent because two wonderful souls met in perfect harmony.

And so, we came to the conclusion that nothing is impossible.

Everything happens with a certain purpose when the time comes.

Robby ... sorry, the writer, finished the second volume. I read it all in a breath and at the end of it I wept with joy.

The rest ... is for you to discover, if you are so curious.

Done Maria-Cristina- alias fairy Crissy

Preface

In fact, my first science fiction was in 1988. I thought I forgot this episode because since then I have focused on poetry. A flight poetry. And yet that 1988 exploded in me exactly in the spring of 2013. Then they were the first laborers to announce the birth of the fantastic novel The Story of a Dream of Love.

Unfortunately, labor was spread over two years because it was only in 2015 to appear. Though the readers' appreciations no longer counted on me, there was a struggle. Something was lacking in this novel. I did not even know what I was not satisfied with.

I raised my bar so high that I decided to make a trilogy starting from the original novel. I drew so loud that the trilogy "Dreaming about Love" appeared with the first two volumes "**The Beginning**" and "**The Coming of the Angels**" in the spring of 2018 in Romanian language..

Then the cherry on the cake followed, volume in English. We launched the exact book in London at **Puskin House.**

Volume III "**Turning to the Light**" I finished it in November 2018, and I was making plans for a launch in 2019. To the question, "What will I find between the covers of this book? " I will answer you as simply as possible.

You will find an ideal, unexpected world where love, peace, harmony want to overcome evil. This trilogy is not only for a certain age because love is not age-aware.

I can not tell you everything because every reader has the right to be found in the trilogy. Prepare yourself unprepared, get ready for something out of the ordinary.

That's not what I'm saying. Robby, Crissy, Nicolas, the fairies, the flowers and all the positive or negative characters.Thanks for wanting to be part of our universe!

Robert Sorin Baicu

Prologue

In my universal consciousness, the glorious blue of the seas was inhabited by many living creatures.

Evolution ... Hmm, I'm going through millions of mental eyes the few monocellular shapes that have developed in the planetary sea and became pluricellular. From those mitochondria to the giant dinosaurs it seems to have passed a millionth of a second.

I wonder if I am the author of all the marvels that seem to have appeared from nowhere on this planet. But there is no one so capable to create them.

Excluding the universal substitution in real space. Is it possible that there are other universes that I, Father, do not have knowledge of? I would have certainly found out... And then why is evolution almost independent of my will?

It is possible that the billions of memories sediment in other consciousnesses, such as planetary consciousness, have been united in a single genetic matrix.

And from the result of all these matrices the free will was born? Probably...

Everything started from the ocean. How fascinated the endless stretch of water. I'm no longer able to contemplate that endless blue that cute me. And yet I decided to add extra complexity.

I wanted to see more than that blue. I was crying, a second later, after that noisy jolt that had started on other millions of planets. And we decided that the dry land was born from the waters.

Plains, hills, and mountains were born from a feverish stirring of my senses thirsty for new knowledge. I did not expect life to attack so furious every millimeter of that dry land I had created in a moment of loneliness.

The children of life, spores, stumbled like small sperm in that muddy egg.

Maroon began to clothe the land with multicolored spots that spread all over like a plague that wanted to capture everything.

Appeared the grass, the flowers of that wonderful color, the huge ferns that would turn into giant trees.

So, the transformation was evolutionary but could also be involutive

Then, in the beginning, everything that was happening was sublime. The greens conquered the dry land, but these states could not stop because evolution is eternal.

The universe itself created by me is in constant evolutionary expansion. I swirled the ocean and felt the waves turn into wild slopes that burst dry. This was my divine sign of calling the creatures from the depths to the dry land waiting for them. The dryness awaited them impatiently. It wanted to give them food, shelter, safety.

And they, the creatures, listened to the call and set off for a new beginning. This challenge pleased them so much that they did not want to leave it. Again, that something came out of my desire.

That's what turned the kings and queens of the ocean into dry knights. It seems like everything's happening too fast. It was impossible.

Maybe I was too eternal to be overcome by that voice of a planet born from simple heartbeat of the Universe?

And yet I was not wrong. We could hear the sweet voice of a blue planet that was bringing children together.

The plants, the birds flying in the clear sky, the marine and terrestrial animals were its children. She was their mother. What I was? Me, the Creator, what I had become?

I felt so offended by this somewhat embarrassing situation that I decided to send the man to that paradise land. I realized too late how wrong I was, but there was nothing left to do.

Perhaps in my secular madness i had embraced the feeling of absolute possession, of the jealousy of self-centeredness that had awakened and wished to be more than a central point. He wanted more.

The master screamed from me, the tyrant who did not want things to get out of control. A false humility drained over an innocent planet, turning the fires into a chaos that would trigger the most terrible curse.

For this self-flagellation to be complete I realized the curse, I felt the Evil being born as a black steam that spread in the universe.

It was a sequential madness that lasted only a second. But, should it have been more? I don’t believe ...The evil in me could not be stopped.

Nor could the curse be stopped.

"You will love this planet, but you will not have it. You will kill it but it will turn into a Phoenix and face you. And you'll kill it again. The curse will last until the worlds unite in Him and Her and the Angels will descend upon your love for the second time ".

Chapter 1

I can't get bored of contemplating. She's so beautiful... Her superbness nudity it thrills me. I feel how it cries, waiting impatiently for my divine kiss

My little one, you'll be blue again the same way as when I got you in my arms for the first time. Please do not hate me for everything I did to you. I told you many times that Evil could eternally enforce you, and you, unknowing and naive, you gave it some monsters that could destroy the whole Universe.

Frankly, I could not afford that risk. I've fallen in love with you since the beginning and believe me I will always love you. I know that this love is more special, that I love in an odd way, but I am too eternal to transform myself. I do not want, and I cannot turn myself into a point in the antithesis of the time. I promise you love and that I will correct all my mistakes and make you happy. Everything will be fine, even if I don't know how I will make it. I'm sure I'll have some revelation, an ancestral sparkle. Something intrigues me!!! Since what started everything?

Oh, I remember. From the madness of a reckless one I had to support to lead all the visible and unseen worlds. My mistake. When I was born the Good, the pain of making was uncontrollable. And all that roar of labor, all the tension turned into Evil.

If I did not cry out my pain and joy, Evil would not have been born. Good and Evil, by their nature, have become antagonistic elements that are constantly warring.

But until this moment, the Azure was born with the rebel, who was about to destroy my entire creation.

If I was not vigilant...but stay, I did not eliminate it. It removed itself. Don’t you believe that’s, love? I cannot believe what you say... love for that earthwoman has eliminated it? But it's a real enormity.

That simple woman, coming from the rebellious homeland, could not take him on the path of perdition. You cannot believe that simple mortals have decided everything. Hmmm, but if I think better everything you say has a logic. Evil has taken possession of my foolish son through Her. That lioness from the rebellious world.

It is possible that evil wished to strike at the mortal who was closest to the Lioness, but, above the understanding, he opposed. Perhaps his spirit was stronger than evil. Yes, it was and is and will be. I read in the book of his life and I realized why he overcame. He was above Death, Fate, above all and everything. I know, in order to prevent conspiracy of the Evil to endanger harmony, I sent an angel. An angel, close to me that stopped everything.

Perhaps this solution was desperate, but I think you understand what it means to be a parent.

Everything are fleeting but leaves very deep traces. My love, I know you're sleepy, but stay a bit longer. I want to tell you something. What? Offf, it's hard. I want to send you the Lioness, I want you to educate her just the way you know it.

Please don’t talk about miracles. You cannot be a dungeon. You are too wonderful. I want you to forget that you are my only lover. Good night!

*

I feel the Father's call ... But why is he calling me? Why exactly me?

Since I was haunting through galaxies? How long has it been? Something tough but unseen is overwhelming me. It's like some chains. As long as I fly nothing bothers me but when I want to rest on a planet, an asteroid or anything else, something is choking me, it gathers me boldly. Why this torture? I am effectively squeezed by powers. I feel the divine punishment through all the pores of my being, though I have not done anything wrong.

I feel like I'm in a nightmare. A terrible nightmare I want to wake up but I can’t. Where am I?

The stars are going so fast next to me, or I'm beside them. Where do I need to go? Why do I feel I have to get somewhere? I can see pictures of the planet that's so dear to me. The planet I have never forgotten. Phenomenal but I haven’t felt like this before. What if it's just a sign of my devastated sense of loneliness?

Perhaps I have come to an end and it gives me the delirium of the eternal wanderers. The images of the arid desert are on the beautiful planet where, once, I have lived long ago? I'm sure the Father wants me there.

And I have to get there at any price. Maybe we have been forgiven, and the ordeal we have lived so far has come to an end. Is it a sign? Possible. I must set my mind in ideas, to temper my motions.

I think it's time to listen to someone. Hmmm, it's so hard to do that. I was accustomed to doing what I wanted no matter if I was wrong or not.

Even though I am, I have not mistaken anything for anyone. I wanted, and I still want... ahh, my whole body hurts me. I want to be The First, to be Alpha and Omega.

Something from another world shouts from me for supremacy. I'm beautiful and smart. I was born to rule and I will do it again because I feel that my desire is the Father's wish.

Chapter 2

Day 1

Ultimately, the purpose always excused the means. I had to do this, which at first glance is despicable, but fortunately it is absolutely necessary.

The woman must reach Terra from one moment to another and once she does, she can’t leave. I will keep her captive until the designer escorts her to her homeland. And not anyway. I have a very pleasant surprise for the others.

I felt too much rebellion in her to hope for a rescue. I have no right to intervene very directly, although there were many ways to eliminate it.

By destroying her soul there was the danger of martyrdom and the seed of rebellion could sprout in the Angel. Knowing my men, this is impossible. Let's not forget that through birth she took something from her and so through an irony of fate to attend to something I do not want forever. The harmony of what we have built so far has to be preserved.

*

Everything looks distressing. I can’t even tell that this is the planet I was born on. Just sand and stones, no trace of vegetation, no trace of life. that I see scares me create a feeling of discomfort.

But eventually it could be worse than that. I could rest somewhere in the Purgatory or even worse, I could've disappeared forever.

I feel the ground under my feet after some time. I should taste every step I take, without having to think so much about all the nonsense that does not help me. I do not know when I'm going to get rid of this sin, so stupid, which makes me to feel bad. The sun is burning ruthless but I somehow feel safe here. My senses tell me I'm safe, but I have to check the surroundings. I do not want to have unpleasant surprises at night.

The lioness was looking up, more and more insistently, the hill that rose not far from her.

It was a high hill but fortunately for her, she found a path that led to the top. She looked at the sky once more and started climbing that path.

As the climb progressed, it became more difficult. She had to rest on the corner stones that were scattered all over. She did not remember to have done this before.

She was breathing harder and harder, with sweat flowing on her eyelids, her throat, all over his body. The first cuts were not delayed, and blood splatters flowed on her palms, marking every stone she was desperately clinging to.

He could not stop from the slope, and he hoped soon to see this calvary end.

At one point she saw on her right something like a cave. Left the trail and started with her last strength moving to what seemed to be the ideal shelter.

Soon she reached the entrance of the cave. Its coolness hurt her unnaturally. Still, this was a prize of her tenacity. It was wonderful this somewhat isolated establishment, which was situated on a position that gave it the possibility of scorching the surroundings without being observed.

She enjoyed the cool place, and for the first time she left all precautions to one side and fell asleep instantly.

"You are the First because you wanted to be. No one in this galaxy can be better than you. I brought you here to be the guardian of this planet I want to wake it up to life.

Remember everything you see and feel because at some point you will need all the information you receive now, here.

When you wake up, you come into the light because my blessing will flow over you. Get it as a new chance to life.

But ...remember!.

Evil perceives you and wants you. It is up to you to resist it. If you do not do that punishment will come upon you.

*

Day 2

Although she was asleep, she felt a strong pressure on the chest. It was becoming annoying, and even if she wanted to sleep, she decided to wake up to find the cause of the discomfort. She gently opened her eyes and looked around. She was alone. She stood up and headed towards the entrance of the cave. Dark clouds covered the sky. Wind gusts swept the desert, picking up the vortices of sand. The visibility was near zero.

Where did those clouds come from? How caused all of this? Finally, it did not matter.

It was going to rain, and that was a pleasure. She enjoyed the coolness, the silence after the rain.

The first peaks were already cutting the dust clouds that receded smoothly to the ground. She left the cave and raised her hands to the sky in a gesture of total abandonment.

The drops of rain were whipping her totally. She remembered the Father's words and thanked him in her thoughts. She felt so free, so relaxed. This rain seemed to wash her soul full of uncertainties.

It was good, that salvation from the high above was sublime. Melancholy was totally covering her. She was thinking of what the future could be ...

Chapter 3

In the mist of the Great Asteroid Barrier, the Crystal Palace dominates over that vast, lifeless stretch. Still, the apparent monotony was broken by the mining conveyors that lurked this land.

Paradoxically or not, magic and logic had their origins here. Origins that were lost in the darkness of times. In the chaos of a multitude of irregular shapes was this world of the two magicians.

Why had they chosen this strange land, why had they turned them into their oasis of silence? No one knew. The point was that the harmony of universal energies was in full accordance with the Laws.

“The Big Azgard Hall ... who ever thought we'd get here ... it’s like a dream.

“Lighten up Nicolas, admire. Admire the greatness of the edifices, their unique harmony.

Sit in the beauty of the people here. Please relax, my dear brother.”

“And yet I cannot believe it. The Grand Master ...”

“Yes, he proposed us to be the defenders of the blue planet of the Milky Way.”

“Will the council accept us?”

“I hope with all my heart. From the short metrics presented is a wonderful planet I fell in love with.

“I agree with you.”

“Do you realize we will be there soon…so beautiful.”

“Yes but…”

Without realizing the two had entered the big hall. Dozens of old people in robes looked at them with the specific severity the initiates had.

Suddenly out of nowhere, He appeared. Judging by the initials on his robe, he was their chief.

“Do you know why you are in this place?”

“Yes.”

“Are you aware of the importance of the mission entrusted to you?”

“We are fully aware of the Grand Master.”

“Would you defend the law and protect this world?”

“Definitely.”

"Then, from this moment, you are the Protectors, responsible for everything that's going on there in that world, at the border of the big barrier. The markings of the Order looked good on their shoulders, and the Grand Master handed them the enchanting rods that would have been their companions undisturbed over time. What times ... and the

years have passed, and here we are, our dear planet is again deserted.

“That's why we are studying the evening writings in the evening, so we can elucidate the hidden enigmas in all the inscriptions and signs.”

“You know Nicolas, maybe what we want to find cannot be found for the time being ...”

“But still…”

''The Lioness is on the new dear planet ..."

"Yes, I know this. We are all, even if we want or not, part of the reconstruction."

"Yet I still feel that I am missing something."

An increasingly violent tremor invaded the Great Hall. The candles were frightened..

A child-like voice could be heard everywhere.

"In October, people will be disguised on Sundays."

Surprised by this unexpected phenomenon, the magicians picked up the wands saying in unison Luminoso Ascende. Everything returned to normal but the two were amazed.

"What was that Nicolas?"

"Do not worry about it, brother, what happened was supposed to happen. Maybe it's a response to the enigmas we want to solve."

"October, people, Sundays ..."

"Wait ... The old man's face lit with understanding. People in the old language would translate to OM. It means Ten, the number of absolute wisdom. Sunday is the seventh day of the week, Father's Day ...."

"So, ten and seventeen ..."

"Woow, turned back is Seventeen and Ten ... this cannot be true..."

"Yes, it is the day and month of the birth of the one who reads beyond the appearances. He was born under the sign of balance."

"Come "Angels and Men''

A small, thin, red-faced book slid off the shelves of the big library and sat down in front of the two magicians.

“Section Seventeen, Paragraph Ten.”

“Unbelievable, look at the titles ...”

“Really?”

“Read more.”

In October, people,
They will dress like Sundays,
And the sun and the universe,
Will be bathed in the feast,
Sweet rivers floating in the worlds of dreams,
When the whisper did not notice,
They will then be transcribed ...

”So. on October 17, the day of the fate.”

“It was...it's not, it's defeated. He is now in the homeland of his ancestors, but the covenant with Terra is strong, so we will find him there.”

"Yes, the myth of the ancient pagans, or rather the Prometheus Initiates, those who have fled from the heights and brought the fire. Robby is part of that.”

“And when the secret whispers ... will be transcribed, zephyrs will fly, it will be spring. In the spring, everything plugs from the frozen claws of death. Life, splendor, harmony.”

“Everything is perfect. So, he will restore balance when dreams will come true.”

“Keep going.”

"But, seasons four,

They will unite in the night,
And there will be two,
In the world of seven,
A warm summer,
And a hot winter,
There will always be this tandem,
And break the spell ... "

“The nuclear winter has devastated our planet so that the axis of rotation has changed. There will be only two seasons. The two hemispheres will have six months of summer and six months of winter.”

“Nothing can change that for now. The poles will be eternally frozen to remind us of the past. It's like a warning.”

“Let's hope this was the last time we witness cataclysms like this.”

Listen…

"And the blond angel,
Coming from unseen worlds,
Will recreate the harmony of his dreams,
He will cover the planet,
In a spell of love,
And sink in the sea,
With his dandelion ".

“So, the blond angel ... gives you this love and hope, light, warmth and tranquility.”

“The Father has saved all those who participate in the reconstruction of the planet. They, in return, have to leave to the descendant’s documents that will become testimonies of the past. These will be a warning and a guide.”

Let's hope that no one ever deviates from the law.

Never, for ever and ever

"And then it will be peace,
From Earth to Heaven,
And evil will perish,
Shuffled, mischievous. "

“But, where is the angel?”

“Nobody has found out where.”

For the second time the magicians were stuck when the little red card began to speak.

”And so, joy,
You will master the world,
That I love,
And I want to forget Pandora,
Bury it in the Sun,
I can connect Terra again,
To the Great Universe."

“As it was to be expected, the key to all enigmas is at Father.”

“Yes, tonight, with his Will we solved a few puzzles. The other question marks will be revealed when time will come.”

"We need to get to the Polus Geticus area to talk to him.

"That's self-evident, but I have a question. The world of the seven. Who are the seven?"

"The seven are actually the seven virtues."

"Goodness of love, truth, hope, modesty, knowledge. All these, allied, give birth to the Absolute Harmony."

Chapter 4

The Lioness delighted looking at the sky. She wanted to find out why she was there.

She wanted to howl her frustration and he wanted to howl his frustration, cast the egotism unmoved to the mute glories that were covered by the clouds, which seemed to hide their future.).

Those clouds coming from nowhere seemed to be threateningly defiant. Her thoughts reverberated throughout the Universe, but she had no way of knowing it. She did not know much, but she wasn't aware of this.

The anger brought them into disbelieving consciousness the disparate memories of the invasion. She wanted resist to these intrusions, but she did not, and that filled her with more anger. A smiling face with the curly hair, the color of the wheat, spiked in her tormented soul.

It induced a state of bliss. This state was multiplying indefinitely.

The condition was painful, at the same time, pleasant). She feel the tears flowing out of her dry and sad eyes)

She put his head in the ground and try with the last powers to remember…

Who was the one who looked like an angel ? Where did she see him?

She lay down on the cold stone with her hands under her head and closed her eyes. She wanted to find an answer to the question that was overfly her mind as a typhoon that had slowly exhausted its powers. It was the first time that this happened to her.

Her? Just her, the invincible by no one and nothing. It was she who, through her serenity and fearlessness, had dominated things, times, men for a long time. And now? What was she now?

She was an exiled, meant to live her cold and tortured eternity on a planet that resembled it altogether)

Something or someone had forced her to realize that those creeds that had shaped them were actually) heresies. They were some fakes that paradoxical or not brought her nothing but pain. Why did she not realize all this? Why now? Why**?** she had accepted willingly to come in this wilderness?

But she had honestly accepted, or just her immeasurable vanity, instilled her desire to be the first one to come to a planet she seemed to know, though she looked different.

In her agitated dreams she saw a green planet with a blue sky ... Or perhaps ... it is impossible ... Father, he would never use the celestial powers to manipulate it ...

Now she realized her dungeon was here. And she could not escape so she had to wait for her judges and the final sentence. She felt that something would happen soon enough.

She didn't know what, but that's what she felt.

No matter how she would have tried to find alibi or subterfuge, she realized that they all have meaning and logic, even if the dice are thrown away. Fate felt hostile, but this aspect made her more anxious and impatient.

As well if this cave, so casually found on her first day on this planet, had become humid, cold, inhospitable.

Everything would end one day, so there was no point in charging her soul with further anxiety.

She stood up and walked into the mouth of the cave. Admiring how the sun was wearing its shining cloak into a cloudless sunset.

The front hill took over the radiance of the rays. Soon will be overnight)

The temperature would drop quite a bit. The sand storms and her anxiety produced migraines, insomnia and depression.

The rain did not leave too long, and the clouds coming from the east once again confirmed this. The giant drops smashed the hot desert with hate. The sound that accompanied each drop of rain was an acoustic sound that irritated Lioness, which was so full of nerves to the maximum)

The sound intensified every single moment more and more. The gusts of the rain lifted a steam curtain that wore the desert in a voluptuous cocoon).

Gathered in one point and driven by an inner thrust into the rain. The rain blew against it, and contrary to all expectations, it felt all this kind of supplication of nature as a release).

All this strange performance became an exaltation of the senses, until it was dizzy, realized that it merged with lightning, darkness, with moisture. The spell of the sands soon took possession of it.

*

"I came…"

The metallic voice reverberated, froze for a second the quiet, pleasant atmosphere of the Great Hall where are the two magicians..

"Robby!! No way ... you are here ... how?"

The man who stood in such a decided attitude in front of the two, smiled.

"I came for you called. Your thoughts, anxiety, and your magical research of things awoke me from the contemplative dawn in which I had found refugee."

"Explain ..."

Robby shrugged for a few moments but mastered crossing his arms. The due respect obliged him to be malleable and compassionate. There was no need to forget who owed it all. Thanks to them, had become more balanced, wiser.

"There's nothing to explain. I was in a meditative area somewhere far. Our energies have come to a common field, and I have realized I have to come to you."

"And yet ... you've changed."

Yes, I was hairless, the wrinkles of the time passed, my eyes were picked by the irritations of the green understanding ... I became what I was supposed to become)

"The Green Precepts of the Ten Initiates, I understand. Feel without having to see. You sacrificed your sight to develop the other senses. According to precepts, this path brings you closer and faster to the Absolute Wisdom of Universal Energies."

"Space-helium lenses are part of me. So, I did not make any conscious sacrifice, it all happened so it was
pointless to oppose this absolutely normal process. As we know, the Ten Initiates are blind, but is the use of two eyes if you don't not feel the thrill of understanding?"

"You have studied very much ... We are happy to you and have reached this stage of knowledge."

"Yeah, I've tried to understand the incomprehension, so I retreated to an orbital station left behind Terra. But close enough to you and the Polus Geticus area."

"You became Ascent."

"Let's say I had to find my Way, eliminate the Evil, and finally seal the deal. I had to become what I am at this moment."

"Your green robe with white and black inlays says it all. You've reached the Final. You know absolutely everything, you are an Initiate."

"Nothing is more wrong. No one, ever knows Everything. Even the Father cannot know absolutely everything ..."

"Blasphemy ..."

The two magicians rose from their chairs, Enlighted the magic wands. Robby stared at them and smiled as a child when he sees a funny toy.

Even if he was disturbed by the somewhat hostile attitude of the two magicians, he did not let that happen, and above
all he did not want to do anything to make himself understood. He was tempted to show his strength, but the Strength in him was stronger than the Evil that was always testing it.

With an extremely careless and bored gesture he called an armchair from the other end of the room. Robby sat down again, still smiling at the two men who stared at him. As if he was the master of that palace he made the two of them to sit down.

“I'm one with the universe I was born of it. I am a drop of energy from an ocean of the Universal Force that obeys the Law.”

“Interesting. According to the old writings there is only one way to reach the Initiate stage so quickly.”

“Namely?”

“Catalepsy. It's that state ...”

“I know, but I still know that nothing is old or new. They are all arranged in such a way that it happens, of course, if all the variables leading to that state of affairs come into the right congruence. All these are ordered independently of our will and our understanding. No matter how we want to change things at some point, it is not possible unless it is time for them to be changed. We believe we have the power to do this, but we are wrong because of our ego that can often be exacerbated. It is true that we can give a nuance to our need of certain secondary aspects. But they all derive from a phenomenon. Only that. God of Non-Entity was not defeated by me alone. And I would not have defeated him forever if the Father did not intervene decisively in this matter, which, if left to chance, could affect the whole Universe. Neither the destruction of the Earth was a hasty action. That is how it was supposed to happen in order to restore balance and harmony to the rightful ones. I didn’t call for this chair just to prove my powers. I called it to me because we had to talk.”

"You know, the course of the time. You know what you need to know."

"Broadly, yes. But let's not forget that this Universe is in a continuous movement and transformation. What we know today and believe is true, tomorrow can be different. It can either be something else or we could see it from a different angle."

"Yes ... perfectly true."

"Often I do not understand the importance of certain information, so I try to stay as long as possible the one I once was. If I would be fully conscious of the Force, it would be possible to trigger a disturbing wave of spatial-temporal linearity.

I'm not a decisive factor as you think. Maybe I'm a simple force of the Force, a force that uses me as much as I use it. Of course, in the interests of good and respecting the Law."

"And yet we feel a little more than what you said."

"Not so far, my dear Nicolas. You are so shocked that you think it's a miracle, a thought of yours, plucked from the darkness of the future. You became for one second one of those primitives in the g7 zones that sees a space shuttle."

"Dear Robby, you get too much infatuation in you and that is why I constrain you to stop having this attitude that is dangerously approaching the dark side of the Force. Do not forget who you are talking to."

"You're wrong again Great Magus. You are enormously tough and extremely heavy. You did not understand anything that I said. You make me believe that all the lesson that you have accumulated over the years fits what I said earlier.

Everything and everything is in a continuous upward movement, but ... it can also be descending.

The wands of the two magicians shone angrily threatening.

Robby opened his eyes, feeling the danger. He realized there was no time for unnecessary lawmakers. He was aware that he could make things well understood, but he did not want to go in an irreconcilable way with his old teachers, who, paradoxically, now has them as subordinates.

He did not want to be aware of this because they felt it and so what he wanted to be a collaboration could become a non-sense. He just confined himself to turning his head to the big library and twisting his eyebrow. Absolutely all the books were out of the shelves and remained hanging.

Disapearo nelegitimis ...

"You cannot do anything ..."

Robby raised his hand and waved his fingers. The wands pointing at him became useless.

"Let's not let things go off. However.!!!"

He stared at the library and smiled, and the books reentered in their places.

"Are you aware that what you did is revolting? You brought us an offense that I do not think we'll ever forget."

"Nothing of a sort ..."

"Silence!!! You do not have the right to speak."

"I'm sorry, but I'll keep talking, no matter if you think you're an enemy or not. I did these things to show you that you, the defenders of this corner of the universe, are touched by vanity. Now,

I wonder if you are a defender or think of yourselves as masters? Maybe it's been too many millennia... but who am I to enlighten you? I wanted to lead your souls beyond the Light, I thought by showing what I had gained, you would be proud of me and you would appreciate it, but as far as I see, I was wrong."

The magicians looked down to the ground, reflecting a few tens of seconds of what Robby said. There was no doubt that they regretted their leaving.

Paradoxically, Robby had shown them a way they were not ready to go. I'm wondering why? They did not know either. Perhaps many millennia had passed, and the continued movement of the Universe had gone unnoticed. This seemed unforgivable, but it seemed to them without doubt that ... yes, the time had come to reorganize the superior mind or ... to withdraw.

Leaving aside all pride, the two stood up and walked to Robby with their arms wide open.

"Forgive us, we are too stressed, and it seems that the burden of liability is already too hard."

It was Robby's turn to look surprised now. He did not really expect such a reaction. He raises to let himself be hugged. Emotions were strong, and they did not foresee that.

However, he wanted to let all these long-forgotten experiences come from the depths of the surface and flood his soul.

It was good, it was that balm he needed so much after a hundred years of self-imposed loneliness.

When you felt that the heartbeats had calmed down, they broke out of their arms and looked at them plainly. They seemed so guilty about the millennia that they felt obliged to encourage them.

“All is well. All's well that ends well. I am with you and ready to help you any problem.”

“Just pray and I hope you do not mind, but we'd like to know more. It is clear that your training can help us.”

“Namely?”

“Can you tell us what is beyond the Light?”

“Surely there is something, but you have to discover it yourself, just as I discovered myself. And yet I will give you a clue as a starting point.”

"I'm surrounded by mist,
What a discrete smell of rain,
Drops of warm light,
They sneak through the streams. "

“Superb, as if it's somewhere beyond Cataclysm, when Good fought with Evil from humans.”

“Listen to the end ...

”And I watch the sunset,
Uniting with a breeze,
I lack the meaning,
Of a world in transformation.
The rain stops for a moment,

Wet, looking at the great horizon
From unseen depths,
Rainbows come out in the sun. "

“Go and explore the Universe, taste its greatness and immensity. Search for the essence. When you find it, think about me. Now I'm going to look for the Angel. It's not yet time to see the Lioness.

With the last words, his face roughed and the pupils narrowed. A rather pronounced grimace allowed to see and to understand several things that it was pointless to say.

Anyway, they all knew Robby's feelings about the Angel's mother.

Chapter 5

Flights fly through dreams.
By telling beautiful stories,
Words speak in parables,
About our fears.

I go through the worlds of eternity,
I am confused with stars that,
Burn unsaid desires,
I burn a magical blow.

Come here, the spotless one,
Because I'm looking for you, where are you?
Come angel,
You are the spell of the stories.

Andromeda, Perseus, Alpha-Centauri Deianeras, Persepolis, Milky Way .. Where would Robby look for the Angel?

The uninterrupted flight through the six constellations and galaxies had terribly exhausted him. He did not really know where to go. And yet he felt he had to find him.

The longing for him was eating him alive, and in all his years of solitude he had not given up his desire to revisit him even if for an instant. He knew that when he had withdrawn himself, it was not the time to see him, but now every cell of his body wanted to feel the one who was his legitimate son in the ancient explorer's spirits.

At one point he felt how everything compress in one point and the movement of rotation of the seen and unseen matter collapsed. He did not understand the phenomenon, but he felt something was supposed to happen. The stars were silently scintillating in unison, then disappeared, and as in a childhood game they appeared elsewhere in his visual perception. He rubbed his eyes and could not believe it. This was just the first-grade novice.

And yet he felt that someone was above him. A melody known only to him was in his head, in his soul, everywhere. Soon, the whole body grew pleasant, and the forgotten sensations revived.
It was like a dream. From nowhere the voice of his son was heard:

I'm here, with you now,
I feel you want to find me,
Do not look for me in the stars,
Search for me in stories.
For I am a dream unleashed from dreams,
I am the lightening,
I cannot measure the eternal,
I'm the second without a rest.

I come and go without a target,
For my home is sand,

There is no time for an hourglass,

I'm your candid zephyr.

Tears poured on his cheeks from the cold of his flights. He raised his hand to wipe them but gave up.

Strangely, but in charm, all such intense exits disappeared as if they never existed. The silence descended into it as a balm. That balm that cured him every time he was in trouble.

*

After that strange and stormy encounter with Robby, the two magicians had long meditated on all things, and had come to the conclusion that their old bones had to be somehow upset.

They were intensely trained for a long journey. But where would they go? They did not know that either. How was that possible? Perhaps the time has come to find out that anything is possible and, above all, they have to understand that they were not unique in solving the enigmas of the universe.

In their higher self, there was a real struggle. Eventually, he had to accept that they were overwhelmed by events.

Later, they declared themselves defeated and climbed into the old tower, opening the Great Star Hall. They had to leave here. They united their wands and called for prayer. It was a prayer for receiving the mission. A huge crystal globe lit up, and from the depths of his eyes, Terra, their dear blue planet.

Now it was just a dead planet.

"Dear brother, even if not even the Father thinks he can do anything for the benefit of this planet, which once was so fertile, I feel it is our duty to get there."

"Let our united forces be strong and manage to bring back this pearl of the galaxy to life."

"What can we do if not even the Father ..."

"Whatever, we owe to try."

The crystal globe turned red. A blazon appeared in the center. The Blaze of the Lioness's family.

Nothing and no one could deny that the Lioness was still a piece of the big puzzle.

"So we have to find the Lioness."

"I feel the solution is in her."

"Why in her? Why not in Antares?"

The Leo's Blaze disappeared, and several shrill lyrics appeared:

"Do not look for me in the stars,
Search me in Stories ... "

"Is that what it is?"

"Stories, myths. Myths of astral explorers. The myth of the Angels. There was evidence in the Aztec region that made it clear that the Anglican people had come to Earth. As you know, they have fallen and merged into the great people of the Mayans, the Incas ..."

"Evidence is found everywhere on Terra, because in that great civilization project there have been at least six major civilizations. The Antares were the leaders who led this grand project. Red people came from Mars ... look for me in stories."

"Now I understand. Angels, stories, Mars."

"We must find the Angel. As far as I can tell, he's on Mars. We need to find him together to get to Terra and find the Lioness."

"Perfect, let's go ..."

The Great Enclave was shrouded in an orange mist. The red mountains were covered with a thick layer of snow that had a multitude of colors. The orange mixed harmoniously with pink and blue and that made ordinary walking through the idea of climbing these mountains through classical methods. It was almost impossible.

The two magicians floated on a cloud, which made their mission easier. The Enclave Sea area is the largest city on the planet.

At this time of the year the climatic conditions were so good that we could say it was summer. Why snow, why that fog?

Something had happened, for as far as they knew during periods of high temperature, fog and snow were inexistent. They found out so much. The purpose they were here was more important than anything.

Even if it sounded selfish, all these aspects were insignificant.

It was important to find the Angel. He felt him in the area they were heading for now.

He entered that pinkish puddle that could hide anything underneath.

The fear of danger is amplified. The view was luxuriant, especially since a cold rain had just started. The buildings, which once again stood imposing in the sun, were now smoking ruins that sheltered terrified shadows that wore their dirty heads.

"God, what happened?"

"It seems that we are uninvited guests in a place where the war is in full swing."

"We need to do something, I do not want to ..."

"Protectoratum ascend!"

A transparent fluid emerged from Nicolas' wand and formed a field to protect them. Clogged blooms were heard somewhere in the outskirts of the big city.

"The more we stay here, the lower our chances of finding the Angel will be."

"Just calm down, I do not like your pessimism at all."

"It's realism ..."

"Okay, locate a hospital or a building that is whole.

"Why a hospital?"

"For, no matter how hard a war is, there is an unwritten law by which hospitals are not attacked."

"If you say so."

"That's right, you'll see."

"Right, we can be there in three to five minutes."

They were two hundred yards from the only building that, like a miracle, had escaped the terror of that war.

"Here's the hospital I was talking about."

"Do you think this is a hospital?"

"You'll convince yourself in five minutes."

As they had guessed it was a hospital.

"I feel he's in the door."

"He is waiting for us."

Indeed, the Angel was waiting for them. Seeing the magicians set aside all precautions, and in his impatient impatience he advanced toward them.

Suddenly, heavy bursts burst out of the right. The killer fire was targeting the Angel because the bursts described had drawn a line diagonally on the asphalt deformed by explosions less than thirty centimeters from him. For a second, he was stuck.

He was actually surprised at what was happening around him at that moment. He sat down on his knees and joined his hands together. All frozen. A total silence covered the conflict zone. He opened his eyes, stood up and walked quietly and smiling toward the Magi.

"Relax, everything is under control, I fell asleep. After all, it is not my war, though its effects may affect this area of the universe in the long run."

"Yeah, but ... why are you here?"

"Fractions in conflict. North and South. The same thing as Terra, but I did not expect the war to break out so quickly and be intense. I participated in peace meetings and discussions. Everything seemed to be heading for a happy end, but a spark triggered the plague. I chose to be in the neutral area taking care of the wounded of both camps."

“Interesting, but you have to go with us on Terra. We have something to do there ...”

“And here? I have to find a solution.”

“There's nothing left to do, no more time. Evil has won. However, this planet is compromised.”

“Let's go then.”

Chapter 6

The vastness of the desert, the sand dunes, the burning sun, and the clouds that stood over the horizon gave a depressing air to the landscape.

The three of them advanced toward the bare hills that stood before them. The temperature exceeded fifty degrees Celsius, so it was more like an oven. A huge, lifeless furnace that everyone else would surely kill.

"Nobody and nothing! And yet, I feel a presence."

"The only being on this planet is the Lioness, Nicolas."

"We're crossing the hills and seeing what we will find."

The two looked at the Angel, who walked impassively alongside. They could not realize the noyan of the experiences that were trying him at this moment. Distorted images that resembled childhood dreams encompassed him, shaking the subconscious.

He is struggling to make connections. Small and large parts of the past slowly joined him. At one point the Angel stopped.

"Alpha and Omega. That's her. But it is not the beginning and the end. It is the Beginning of the End. She is my mother."

"Right, you're right kid. Let's go. We're glad you came to this conclusion alone."

Soon they had arrived at the hilly formation that arose as a bastion that majestically guarded the vastness of the desert. The terrain was extremely rugged, and it was sprinkled with huge granite blocks. Where they came from was a real mystery, but that did not interest them at the time.

They wanted to climb that hill that attracted them like a magnet, but they did not manage to find a smoother slope. They knew that the Lioness was here. They felt her presence, but they could not see her.

She did not show up, so they had to look for it. Indeed, the Lioness was not going to meet them. She didn't want that now. She was watching every move they made from somewhere above, trying to figure out what had brought them to her area.

These strangers awakened her with a strange feeling coming from the depths of her soul. She seemed to know them, as though ... and that kid with yellow hair ... His soul was full of this image. The whole being had focused on the serenity of his eyes. Where and when did she meet them?

Strange feelings, like some obscure memories come into her traumatized consciousness of loneliness. She felt a state of well-being and guilty embarrassment. She threw all these perceptions somewhere on the edge of consciousness and resumed observation. The three were getting closer and closer to her shelter. Was it good for them to discover her home?

Without going through the filter of the mind, she jumped before them.

"Hello gentlemen. How can I help you?"

The unexpected appearance surprised the three. After a few seconds of scrutiny, they turned to the Lioness who was watching them impassively. And yet she could feel the tension she was holding at that moment.

"Hello, can you help us? Of course, if you want ..."

"I'm particularly curious to find out how."

"It's simple, you can look into yourself and figure out how to do it."

"Hmmm, an interesting answer, but I think there is no time or place for such an "exercise." Or maybe I do not have time for that."

"Irascible and defiant as usual. I might think you have not changed. My dear, you do not have to make yourself uncomfortable. We do not want to do you wrong."

"Something strange urges me to trust you, but ..."

The wands of the two magicians emerged from their wide sleeves, and they climbed into the air uniting themselves. A green wave was born out of that connection, and in less than a second the Lioness awoke trapped inside a translucent field. She slid fainting in the dust. The angel scowled and turned toward his mother.

"Stop it, nothing happened to her."

"But ..."

"Now she will remember who she is, where she comes from and who we are."

"Perfect, but I hope it does not last long."

"It's done. Disapearo."

The translucent field vanished, and the Lioness opened her puzzled eyes.

"What was that?"

“Nothing special, I answered your questions.”

“When the three of them meet the blue planet, will wake up to life.”

“Yes, the writings do not lie.”

“I saw a man with ascetic face, bald, athletic figure, and you were there blonde traveller.”

"Yes, this is your son, and the ascetic man is the man who was your husband, the father of this wonderful young man.”

“Interesting.”

The Lioness rose and approached the Angel. She gently lifted her hand and stroked him, staring at him. A soft smile appeared on the Lioness’s face.

“You're my son down from the stars, and you are the Defenders of the Blue Planet. Now I know, I remember everything.”

She remembered that separation, his childhood and the cataclysm. Then the Father and his voluntary participation in this experiment on a deserted planet that was shaken by endless sand storms.

For the painting to be even more lugubrious, even for her, the temperatures were too high. Now she seemed to feel a liberation. She felt that her role in this story had come to an end.

“Finally, all this madness will end. I'm glad because my guinea-pig role in an unsuccessful experiment stops with your coming.”

“Maybe it does, maybe it doesn’t.”

“Okay, then I'll let you have a great day.”

"Stay, where are you going? You can help us find the gateway to Antares."

"How?"

"It seems that you are the only one who can find this gate. Dig deep inside of you and find what you need."

"As I see, I have such valences too."

"Nothing is accidental ..."

"Ok, I'll come with you."

The magicians smiled and started walking after the Lioness. They did not really expect a collaboration with such a difficult being. And yet she had to find the gateway to Antares.

"Where does this lead?"

"To a cave. I live there."

"Oh, let's go."

It was too good to be true. Could the gate be there? Based on all the probabilities, it should be there. They had scoured the papers, and according to the calculations they were near.

"Will we make a trip to Antares my lords?"

"I do not think it can be possible. Anyway…"

The lioness suddenly closed her eyes and entered a kind of trance. They all stopped waiting for her to come back.

"He has to come to the gate ... another exile. I'm wondering why? For what? What am I wrong with? Tell me!"

"Only He can give you the answer."

"I was sure. I felt his warmth and his coldness, I felt the good and the hate. I felt and watched the story unfold."

“Unbelievable, so you woke up.”

“Yes, I know what awaits me, the past, the present and the future have joined me.”

“It's okay then.”

“But who are you for I can’t see you anywhere.”

"You cannot see me because I am Grand Magician Nicolas. They are everywhere because I and this fellow are the Defenders of this area in the Milky Way Galaxy.”

Chapter 7

Once upon a time, it was called the Blue Planet, now, it was just a simple heavenly body where the yellow was joined with that grey tern. When it was created you could easily say with slight envy that this planet was the pearl of the Creator, because never, anywhere, it had not provided a planet with so many wonderful, beauties.

No place in this galaxy could meet a similar planet that has so much lush vegetation, so many forms of harmony fused together. Rapid rivers, lakes, seas, oceans were everywhere inhabited with a great variety of living creatures. On land the flora and fauna were so diverse that you could swear you were in a paradise. All the symbiotic-chemical processes formed that barrier that protected the planet from solar radiation. Like you said that all plants and creatures are actively involved in maintaining life. Maybe that is true. And yet there was something missing to make the difference.

Though the other worlds had expressed the desire to protect this paradise by wanting to be just a touristic point, those in Antares had advanced a civilization project to the Great Wise Men. Following stormy debates lasting more than two months, the project received a green light. The only clause was that at least six civilizational centres actively participated in the Terra3 Reconstruction operation of the Book of the Third Blue Beginning.

"Nice but ..."

"But now focus on what I gave you to do. Disconnect the pilot automatically and report the data."

“Wow ... we are in the Milky Way Galaxy's perimeter, biometric systems are activated, and I expect from one moment to another to get information.”

“Very well ... continue with the advanced monitoring channels.”

“Perfect.”

Maybe for convenience, perhaps not to waste the energy he needed so much, Robby, got on the ship that had been waiting for years on the special plateau behind the residence on the planet Falixera.

Now he had awakened from meditation perhaps because he had felt close to the planet he loved so much. How long since he left his native planet? Very long.

One month ago, he had been given the mission to reach Terra. He was not interested in who received this order. He was not the kind to consider insignificant aspects. However, there were very few people who could give him tasks.

Mission details were important even if they did not have them at the time. He knew they would come at the right time.

The flight itself could take between four and six earth days, but at standard light speed it took about two days.

He had chosen these parameters to enjoy in silence the landscapes offered by the immense complexity of the Universe. He liked the idea of making a one-day stopover on one of the relaxation centres, but had quit.

The mission seems to be of major importance. Safety and identification procedures were required that at the entrance to the galaxy, the Flight Monitoring Centre should be notified of the purpose of the visit. He had typed a Q1 and is still reading History. An old, thick manuscript covering all the important events of the great civilization empires. There were only a few copies in the Great Library on Falixera.

The Protectorate High Rank gave him the right to access any information. There, in the Great Library, he had a small room on the ninety-fourth floor. Here he received his friends and he also attended video conferences. Systems in conflict of interest, ratifications of the new laws issued by the Grand Wise Council and much more.

He had recently counselled the conflicting state of the major industrial conurbations on Mars. He was not the only conciliator. Surprisingly or not, the Angels Order had delegated his son to take part in the discussion.

Of course, he did not know what interests they had in the area, but taken the fact that the civilization centres had the right to take notice, it was normal for him to take part.

After the debate he searched for his son and had been with him for several hours. He had matured too early, but he was not scared because he knew his gene was extremely strong.

He would gone soon on Mars to prevent escalating tensions accumulated in a relatively short time.

For a second, Robby had gone through his head to join his son in all these actions, but felt he had to go somewhere else. He could not read the future but broadly, a future that was constantly changing, so he did not know how close he would be to his son or soon, even very soon.

"Drone reports ..."

"Listen."

"Fifty-nine degrees Celsius temperature, nocturnal temperature -fourteen degrees Celsius. Sandy storms, heavy rains accompanied by frequent electrical discharges. Forms of life: three. Oxygen flow in normal parameters from water evaporation, concentration ..."

"(Enough) Hold on, please, the (observation).. Act your security systems when you enter the atmosphere and release drones to capture extra information.

So it was not Antares. No ship is in the immediate vicinity of the planet." Who were the three? He would find out in the next few minutes.

"Portal location in the northern hemisphere at forty-five degrees of the centre belt."

"You mean the Equator. I told you to do the translation of language. I can't stand the official academic faculties even though I was a lecturer."

"I understand."

"Scan the area in depth. I want a variable temperature spectrum."

"According to the analysis required in the third section is the Plateau of Transylvania."

"Triangulates and intensifies spectral points."

“Three subjects. As far as I can see, there is the Gate there.”

“Perfect, land in the area. Provides perimeter and enters stasis.”

“I understand.”

Robby descended from the ship, stared around, nudged the air filled with sand particles, then teleported into the area of action.

*

"High Council, our observation probes have detected two ships landing most likely on Earth. We also monitor the conflict area of sector four, Mars, through observers.”

“We have known all of this and thank you for your actions. It has always been a great pleasure to work with you.”

“We have information on a possible intervention in the theatre of operations on Mars.”

“Yeah, this manoeuvre is not a secret, and I think we'll do it as the Terra 2 – Finish mission. The last observer of the Angels left for Terra two days ago.”

“I noticed this, Great One.”

“We're waiting for a video conference. There will be five civilization centres. Of course, you are special guests, given the significant contribution you have as a civilization centre. After the conference, regardless of the decision to be taken, I will be especially honoured to continue the discussion that unfortunately ends now, honourable Coudius.”

Coudius, the Ambassador of the Antares to the High Council, touched his chest and sketched a slight bow, then turned to the door and left the room.

The sly ambassador was aware of the video conference, the subject of the talk, of everything that was happening in that world.

What he did not know was just the result of those discussions, but it was certainly the one he guessed. His spies were of extraordinary efficiency, so he was aware of all the events.

Now he was in a hurry to get to his apartment to attend the video conference that was about to begin soon.

One fact intrigued him. Why was he not informed, why was not an official invitation made?

For the moment, he forgot about this. He mentally ordered his servant to prepare all the necessary videoconferencing. He crossed several corridors and then teleported into his favourite armchair.

The meeting was about to begin. The Great One was making presentations. There were those from the Alpha Centauri, Perseu, Andromeda, the Order of the Angels.

Casiopeea also attended the meeting, and of course, as observers, those in the Milky Way.

"Gentlemen, I am glad and at the same time I am particularly honoured by your presence at this meeting. Let me remind you that the themes dealt with are of particular importance. As you know, undesirable events have disrupted universal harmony. Evil elements have broken the laws."

"Both me and my colleagues are aware of these events in the smallest detail. Please tell me your point of view and what immediate steps must be taken so that the situation does not degenerate."

Coudius hates excessive diplomacy. He was a practical, incisive type that emphasized the value of the facts.

He himself hated those in the Council. He hated their foolishness and the mildness of the words that he throws into the wind.

He knew that those in the Council had similar feelings about him, but they had nothing to do about it. It was a necessary, extremely necessary evil.

"Unfortunately, we will intervene with force, we will extract the positive elements from the theatre of operations, then we will eliminate the conflict outbreak"

"Easy Great Wise. You are saying these things as if they are already decided. Why did we get together?"

"Forgive me, honourable Coudius but the events are precipitating. I know that an ultra-separatist faction wants to activate the mass destruction systems and then withdraw to Terra."

"I have understood very gravely this issue, but we need to look at the stages. Without a well-planned plan, any operation is doomed to the failure from the start. That is why I will ask my colleagues to vote for the points I will put on the right of the screen. Discussions are no longer relevant, given, as you said, limited time."

All participants voted. The Great Wise was visibly annoyed by the fact that Coudius took the initiative of discussion. Realizing the danger of being removed from this meeting, he tried to save his reputation. He had to remain the centre of attention at any price.

"Gentlemen, after seeing the resolution, was unanimously approved. We move on to point two. Earth situation. As you know, this planet must be brought back to life. First phase...

"Thousands of Great Wise Excuses. But what is the reason why this is required? Why should she be brought back to life? We know with all what happened and what bad consequences followed when the earthly civilization has become irreversibly contaminated by the force of Evil. I think it is better to leave it as it is today. I think everyone here agrees with me."

"Honourable Coudius, I do not think you want to challenge the decision-making power of the Supreme Fora. The Terra Planet has a strategically highly sensitive position, so we want to repopulate it regardless of your position. If distinguished ambassadors do not agree with this, we will look for other solutions and contact other systems that want to participate in the civilization of this planet."

"So let's see… we have no choice ..."

"You are the most prolific civilizations and that is why I chose you for this grand project, but if you do not want to participate nobody can bind you."

A shadow of dismay passed over the faces of all the participants. The situation was embarrassing. It never occurred to the Supreme Council to shadow the vanity of luxury civilians at least.

That's how they used to call them. But, here, today, someone had the guts to impose that was right, a big project. They were suspecting that it's more then what we can see but there was no reason to get into a dispute with the council. The situation could've gone downwards for sure.

The projectors started to turn off one by one.

Only the Earth's representatives, Coudius, the Ambassador of Antares, and the Order of the Angels remained active.

"Understand that the others refused the project?"

"Yes, as far as I can tell. I think it is an extremely costly project that has a very low long-term success rate."

"Gentlemen, considering that you are the only one you are here now, I take it as an acceptance of participation in the two projects?"

"Yes and no ... from my point of view."

"Explain yourself, honorable Coudius."

"Considering the complexity and scope of the two projects, I want to withdraw to discuss with my officials and superiors. Following the discussions, I can give you a firm answer. I believe that my distinguished colleague, Benedictus, will do the same."

"Then I'm waiting for a reply within one hour. If this answer does not come, I will contact other civilization systems."

"Agreed."

Coudius jumped with ecstasy. Even in his most beautiful dreams he would not have dared to believe he would remain alone at the table. Finally, the third and fourth areas of the Milky Way galaxy were theirs. The Antares Empire widened its area of influence.

The superiors would be extremely pleased with his work. He even expected himself to be a great protector and Governor.

He had no way of knowing that fate had left him some surprises.

Extremely spicy surprises. Now it was only about how hard these super sights could be. The highly sensitive and refined stomach was ready. Could he resist?

Chapter 8

The group advanced to the top of the hill on a twisted roar that sneaked like a huge snake among the huge blocks of stone.

Suddenly, in the sky that was now unmistakably clear, there appeared a black dot that fell speedily.

The entrance to the atmosphere did not ignite it, but it gave it reddish inflections, which showed that the strange object was not immune to the high temperatures caused by air friction.

The Lioness noticed the first phenomenon and stopped.

He followed with interest the crossing object. In fact, it was not an object. It was a space shuttle. At one point, the steering propellers came into operation. The small ship described a circle arch and lowered silently somewhere in the front of the hill.

"What was that?"

"I'm sure it's a visitor. As I saw that object looked like a ship. It was in perfect condition, so it's not an accidental incursion."

"Maybe Nicolas, anyway we have to get over the hill to see what he is, or better to say who he is."

"So, we'll see who he is?"

"Not yet possible. They left in the evening and we don't know how long we have to go to the Lioness's shelter."

The lioness looked at them screeching and shuddered as if she had been electrocuted.

"Is He ... I felt it."

"Who is he?"

“It is him.”

“He and Her ... Is it Robby?

In response to their perplexity, the hill shines and Robby appears in front of them.

“Yes, it is. I am glad to meet again.”

He took a hard look at the Lioness, then, walking past, headed for the Angel that he took in his arms. Then he hugged affectionately with the two magicians.

“My dear boy, we'll have enough time to talk. Now head to the cave at the top of this hill. There is the portal that links us to Antares. We have to hurry. I have information that shows that things have gone wrong, so we have to get to Antares as soon as possible.”

“Yes, of course, we have the Lioness can open it ...”

“Unfortunately, Lioness is no longer the key to Antares. My son has been automatically transferred these prerogatives.”

“Perfect, then let's go.”

The Lioness smiled enigmatically, as if distracted by everything that was going on. Passing beside Robby, she whispered,

“The beginning and the end do not exist anymore.”

“Why do you think that?”

“Because I am All. I am the substitute of the Father.”

“What you say is an aberration. If what you say is true I'm telling you that the problem has changed. You are no longer a substitute.”

“Why?”

"Because I came out. Sometimes fate is in danger and it makes partial mistakes to the simplest problems. Paradoxically or not, we, those who are the Defenders of the Laws, direct our mistakes to restore harmony and peace. Nobody is Everything for the simple fact that we are part of Everything."

"Anything is possible."

Robby stopped from the storm to the crest of the hill, took the Lioness's face in his hands and, looking deep in her eyes, said:

"Your role in this piece is over. It's time to leave the scene. Obey and cast out your pride that has made you so wrong in the past. Try to fix as much as possible, anything that can be repaired, otherwise you will regret it. Even the

Angel will not be able to save you. The place of your spiritual propitiation is with no return. Believe me, I saw that with my eyes a while ago."

"You've always liked to be brave ..."

"Wrong. But in the end, I'm not here to give you explanations. The time of explanations and contradictory talks has passed. Get behind me and try to resist your useless sarcasm."

He continued the climb, which was not so difficult, perhaps because the slope had grown lighter. Soon they reached the entrance of the cave. Robby signalled to the others to stop.

"Get behind me and whatever happens, stay there."

"Why? It's my house, there's no danger."

"I once asked you to supress your impulse. Now I force you to shut up."

"You do not have that right. I'm First, and so I'll stay forever, so ..."

"You are but .... being of the rebellious. You do not have the right to speak."

Robby raised his hand and said a simple Silencer. The Lioness flushed all over and remained quiet. She could not speak anymore.

"If you do not calm down, I may as well immobilize you Anyway, after we finish the job here, we will have a very nice and instructive discussion. I, You and the Angel.''

Robby raised his hands to the sky and closed his eyes. The profound incantation enveloped the walls of the cave, in sand in the air. In fact, it was not a magical chant. It was a prayer to the forces of the universe:

It's our story,
Come here where you are,
You are the bright way,
To Heaven's sight.
You are detached from the rebellion,
And burning seed,
Your mother is a sentence,
I am a traveling ray.

Out of that spell, the angel grow huge white wings coming straight from his shoulders. His dark blonde hair became brighter and brighter, yellow as wheat spikes. His eyes were blue and he was surrounded by a huge aura.

Prayer continues more fierce, deeper, more reverberating. Stone blocks vibrated sharply, describing a motion down the hill. The angel had risen above all, immersed in a meditative state.

I invoke you to come out of dreams,
Open the world way,
It comes down from the story,
A sweet love that hurts.

The silence re-joined, easily, smoothly, without any force. In fact, it was the silence before what was going to happen.

Nicolas said something, but Robby stopped him. It just seems like simply forcing him to be patient. He looked away and obeyed. The angel descended to the ground, continuing to pray for his father's prayer.

I come as an angel of sweet dreams,
For a dream of dreams is,
Softly coming down from the constellations,
Wake up this earth.

There was a roar in the distance. Sandy trumpets rose to the sky in a dizzying dance. Strong air streams chained the Lioness and lifted her up to heaven, carrying her in an unknown direction.

The cave had disappeared in a miracle, and the Portal appeared instead.

"The desert has become a fertile soil, and somewhere to the north stands, the sandy Mountain. That's where the Lioness is."

"So, the Reconstruction begins."

"It depends on what the Antares people say."

Chapter 9

Even though she had seen dozens of planets, of which the most beautiful, the green algae with blue iris fascinated them. On the stretched plain, the flowers and the helixander bush gave a special note to Antares's landscape. Deciduous forests were surrounded by three splendid plains. There were snow-covered mountains that sank in the light of the suns to a warm pink. In front of them was the great metropolis of the Antares Empire.

The two magicians, Robby and the Angel, headed for the city gates. They knew their arrival had not gone unnoticed.

They were expecting to be spotted from one moment to another by the security drones.

They were delayed. Instead, he could see three transport ships flying over the area where they were.

“Let's stop, though. There has to be a delegation.”

“Is this the protocol?”

“Yes of course. The protocol is very strict on these lands, so there is no point in going forward. It could be misinterpreted.”

Robby knew the best of the Antares. Many years ago, he had spent some time here.

He was still a novice in the conciliation policy, and the Anthurians were famous for being able to solve the most tangled situations.

The three ships landed in front of them. In fact, there were two small surplus shuttles and a larger protocol aircraft. The protocol ship trap opened, and four people emerged from the inside, who appeared to be magistrates by appearance and clothing. Robby recognized Coudius, who was mumbling in the front.

The richly ornamented garments and jewels of fashion on Antares showed without any doubt that he was supposed to be the head of the delegation. Robby, the Angel, and the two magicians came forward to them.

"Welcome to Antares Earth people. It is a real honour to meet the Earth Defenders."

"Well, we found you honourable Coudius, I was wondering who would meet us."

"High Prelate, on what occasion on Antares? I knew you were on Falixera."

"I am everywhere they need me so I'm here now. I came from Terra."

"Why Terra?"

"Because it's the planet that once, long ago, I civilized, it's the planet I was born on. Because of this, I chose to bring it back to life regardless of whether I am helped or not."

"You're amazing. You've fascinated me all the time. You have something special that impresses me."

"Thank you for your appreciation. We came here to discuss important issues related to the future of the Earth. I understand that the High Council has given the right to restart the reconstruction of the planet."

"Perfectly true, but some details need to be dealt with. The project is far-reaching ..."

"I know that, that's why we'd like to take part in the talks. As official representatives of the planet, we want to hear and agree on every aspect."

"I agree with that, but we also need to find the High Council opinion."

"Coudius, do you think I do not know about the appreciation you enjoy. Do you think I do not know what influence you have?"

"To make your way easier I invite you to my ship. I will give you the necessary instructions for your stay in the capital to be as enjoyable as possible."

Coudius, of course, had the ability y to manipulate discussions of any kind in any direction he wanted. He was slightly amazed by this Prelate who had once been a student. He hated himself for underestimating him. He had left his guard down and had received an unexpected blow. Many times, when the victory over the direct opponent was left waiting, he consoled himself with the thought that diplomacy had its secret ways.

Coudius hoped to somehow rebuild the wrong little step that had made in a moment of exuberance. But what was wrong with him? The senses had warned him of the arrival of these Venetians who were abolishing the title of Earth ambassadors. He had ignored his senses because vanity had shaded the logic of things.

But how did the Prelate know so many things about him? Had his paranormal capabilities been superior to his? He knew what nobody knew.

Oh, his last success had brought him so many titles and benefits that he had forgotten the efficiency of his own thinking. Now he realized that he relied more on his army of spies than on his own judgment. That army had only reported in passing information on the Terra situation. And he did not care about this because he was sure that planet would return. He dreamed that he would be the sole master, and shortly thereafter, independent of all the snobs believed to be all-powerful gods.

He did not have the necessary information about the Three Theatre Operations. The situation became more embarrassing when he realized he didn't have up-to-date information about this mysterious character.

But what could he discover in a man who could not be scanned in any way.

Why did not he send people to find out more information? Something or someone did not allow him to take a close look at some aspects.

Information, information and information. That was the top of the hierarchy. He always had the ability to turn information into intrigue, being always one step ahead of others.

He knew something was not connected in this whole story, so he had to be extremely cautious from now on.

His sincerity about such an important problem proved to be uninspired. Was his silence a better thing? Or maybe he had to deny it vehemently. Realizing that anything he tried was superfluous.

Anyway, these strangers were here, and they had to play as they were singing.

The Supreme Council of the Antarian Empire had met in an extraordinary session.

Discussions were to take place only on the edge of a single point. Implementation of state-of-the-art technologies on Terra and Mars.

This Antarian Council was chaired by Grand Lord Chancellor Sor-in Rob.

Robby had heard of him but had never met him. He had participated in many military expeditions and it was known throughout the galaxy that his decorations and deeds of bravery were not scornful. He was really impressive. The more than two meters he had, defied the whole room. She was dressed in a simple purple robe without any modern jewellery. His look said he was not the kind of politician who took into account the canons of his cast. He liked to be short and to the point.

"Honour your colleagues, honoured Earth delegation, as you know, we discussed all the stages of the project that includes both the Three and the Four. We agreed on the way in which this will take place. It is very important to know how much we want this project to become achievable, because there are two currents. Some want to revive that part of the galaxy, others do not. Now I ask you as the only representatives of all and I want your vote to answer this question. Do you want these two planets to remain just some tourist attractions for the whole universe to enjoy, or do you want your hard work to be rewarded one day by those you are helping? Think well and take into account the beneficial strategic partnership if cataclysms or wars will hit this empire. We have enough hostile systems that are just waiting for a wrong. The Three and Four Systems may be the allies we need so much. "

Disapproval mixed with frenetic applause.

The Grand Chancellor smiled. He knew that the passion characterized his race so that the talks could continue infinitely without the immediate vote. He was the declared partisan of the reconstruction and he was proud of his position within the community. The only direct descendant of the Bai Antarians had a strong support on most of the empire's planets.

As well as he was seen in most of the circles that frequented were his opponents. These were not simple people. They were the descendants of old families, particularly fluffy. Among his most influential and dangerous was his good friend Coudius. The Grand Chancellor knew this. Although he had tried to draw him on his side, he remained in the expectation of the one who weighed the advantages, but especially the disadvantages.

Sor-in-Rob knew that Coudius was avid for power but still did not want to throw a serious offer until the Conservative Party had decided on a viable strategy.

Anyway, in their last meeting, Coudius had stepped in to the fact that he would be particularly honoured to give him the position of governor and the title of Lord Commander. Now he would find out where the balance would be inclined.

Sor-in-Rob also considered the neutral element. Instead of another adversary, it's good to have a neutral person.

Throughout their stay they had studied the four Earth representatives. He was amazed at the fact that he had failed to discover much. Only truncated information, which, gathered, gave no concrete clue to the psychological side.

He had unlimited access to any source of information, whether classified or not, but found nothing relevant. Central Supreme Council information, their appointments as official representatives of the Territory, the last places of residence, but so much.

He could read the High Prelate and the Anglican Order representative as much as possible, but the two elders were a total enigma. Who were and what they were doing here did not know anyone.

He could still feel that these two were trustworthy. After two intense voting sessions the votes were fifty-fifty and only one person didn't vote.

It was predictable that Condius would not vote. He was waiting for offers. Whoever offered more would win the battle.

Before leaving towards the four representatives, Sor-in-Rob sent through an agent an offer no one could refuse. It was an official declaration signed and stamped obeying all the rules.

*

Robby admired the moons that guarded Antares, and from time to time he sent his spirit to the heights to be as close to this splendid view that unfortunately had to leave soon.

The magicians were in the next room, whispering the latest events. The angel ... The angel was not in his room.

Probably the capital is going to admire the superb architecture of the buildings.

Robby felt almost instantly the presence of the Angel behind him. He stood for a few moments then turned to smile at him. He could not afford to read his thoughts.

He wondered from where he walked. He smiled seriously in his turn and rubbed his finger against his lips. An enigmatic smile that told Robby that his boy had not gone on a simple walk.

He was glad the young man had learned to value, the information. He knew the security systems that, even if they were forbidden by the Universal Rights Charter, were widely used unofficially, especially in the capitals of the great empires.

They were being monitored and listened, so they could not speak. He approached the Angel and took him as naturally as possible.

They were in an unsafe and hostile world. Lazy smiles and simian politeness hid hatred. This was the unseen face of the wonderful capital of the Antares Empire.

"Read what it takes and act."

"I understand."

Chapter 10

He was watching and could not believe it. It was terrible what could happen in a room where so many people who thought a superior race were screaming, threatening to push themselves out of all sorts of offenses that made them dirty. Are these those who were to civilize Earth?

He had to gather more information. This was necessary because tomorrow would be too late. He felt he was looking at an insistence he could not overlook.

He discovered a group of three men who were intensely analysing him. Feeling uncovered, they moved their eyes, then engaged in a dialogue with a man who joined them.

Nobody other than Coudius, who, in that storm of pro and contra vote, was a very discrete presence. He raised his gaze to the Angel then told the others. All four were heading for the exit.

He had nothing to do but to pursue them in order to know their intentions. He did not believe in coincidences.

The hostile eyes of those people were telling a lot. So much to feel that something rotten is about to happen.

The angel closed his eyes, concentrating on Coudius last image imprinting it on the retina teleporting. Would someone find it missing? Luckily not. His energy curtain was dematerialized in three hours.

He woke on the edge of a lake surrounded by a forest. The steep slopes were sprinkled with beautiful stone blocks. Nearby he saw the four standing in the circle. They came close to them to decipher the discussion they had. He enveloped himslef in a protective aura that would keep him from being discovered and come forward until they were two feet away from them.

*

“Gentlemen, I am honoured that this evening we can speak freely and openly about certain determinant aspects of my political future.”

“Your future?”

“My future is your future.”

“In view of the current conditions, we want to learn as much as possible about the action plan.”

“It goes without saying that everything we talk about here remains secret and ...”

“We are honourable men, and we have a word, so you do not act as if you had some sort of thing in front of you.”

“Life taught me to be extremely cautious. Any indiscretion in this extremely dangerous game can cost someone's life ...”

“It is a matter of course. If I was not perfectly aware of this, I wouldn’t have been here tonight.”

"You Xelonimus and the other jurors on Sortalya and Matiyoia that you keep your secret and that whatever happens would you blindly follow my orders?”

“We swear.”

"From now on we will forget our names and we will only use numbers One, Two, Three and Four."

"An excellent idea."

"The plan is simple. If those who are against the colonization of the Earth are victorious…"

"If... you said that right."

"Shut up and listen. If the winners come out, then we will assassinate them on the representations of the Earth and by diversion we will all blame them. There will be the chaos fed by us, until the shadow of a civil war will appear threatening and hideous. We will force early elections. If this plan fails, the coup is the last card we'll stake everything on."

"If the vote is favourable to us?"

"Then everything is perfect. I will get to Terra and I will call you continental governors."

"Let's hope Fate will be on our side. I honestly do not mind the idea of getting closer to Earth people. Something tells me they are extremely dangerous."

"Let's go back to the hall now. My presence cannot go unnoticed to infinity. I'm the man who can make a difference."

"Perfectly true."

The four men left the place, and the Angel looked blank. In what moral world had he landed? He could not believe it. Even in the most fanciful dreams he would not have imagined that some of the pillars of an extremely advanced society could indulge such a vanity. He sighted, closed his eyes and teleported.

*

"Good evening, gentlemen, unfortunately tomorrow you have to leave us. We never agreed to the Protocol, but that's it."

"It has been a great pleasure to meet you, to find out that we have such important friends who want evolution to be in perfect harmony with the spirit. You are wonderful people with an amazing living standard."

"High Prelate I hope to see you as soon as possible under more favourable conditions. Anyway, I, Lord Chancellor Sor-in-Rob, from the great nation of Bari Antarians assure you that I will not spare any effort and will do everything possible to bring the Earth among the civilized worlds."

"I hope that..."

"I do not want you to hope for anything, you have to take this promise of mine as a certainty."

However, this evening everything will be decided, and I am absolutely sure that this great project will be accepted.

"I understand."

"I do not know how much you know, but there's a serious disturbance in the area that interests us both."

"I know more than I can say. I am about to solve this problem that concerns me directly."

"I'm sorry that this issue is so directly concerned, but my sources ..."

"Sources are ineffective. I heard this tonight. You do not continue, it's pointless for someone else to know what we just know."

"No worries, I'm ready, I'm not a novice. No one can sneak through my shield."

"Then we can talk quietly. Listen. And I hope you listen to me later. I have something very important to tell you. Something extremely serious."

"Let's get everything right. First of all, the Lioness will have to return to her ancestral home, more precisely in the Gothic Worlds. As you know, those worlds have never adhered to the norms of the Laws. No matter the details, it is certain that this young Angel will take her there and take care that the Dark Force in her does not develop."

"Probably not. Especially because it is in a bad area."

"Great Prelate this young man has some extraordinary qualities. I did not think that under such an innocent face there was such a penetrating mind."

"Young man, I totally trust you. If possible and if you have the ability to eliminate that force, please do it. It's for everyone's sake. If we fail the fate of the Worlds, will be sealed. No one, even the great Prelate, can do anything else. But hopefully everything will be fine."

The angel listened, but beyond this discussion he was already thinking about the journey to his mother, who had to be exiled away. He did not even know where the worlds of the Lord were. The context and the sentence had taken him by surprise, so the logic of things escaped him. He sighted, shook his shoulders and said:

"I will carry out the task and I will do my best to return everything to normal."

"Normality is a word, an ambiguous state that differs from individual to individual. Every man has a well-defined set of rules and beliefs that make him good or bad. The worst is when you get between two precepts and you want to get them together. Good and evil cannot coexist. Finally, you have to stop and choose. Going after chimeras is not the right way. Be good, respect and obey the Universal Law, or you will become the slave of Dark Forces."

"Paradoxically or we cannot find it the other way around. Those who serve evil say the same thing, and thus antagonism is born."

"Perfectly true, I do not think it is beneficial to waste our time with discussions that are now useless. You will go and stay there until you are sure that darkness and pride and egocentrism have disappeared from it. May the Light and Truth accompany you everywhere.

"Before you do, I have to do one thing. This is what my father will tell you. But not here and not now. All I can say ... The best friend is the hottest enemy. This night is full of dangers."

The angel closed his eyes and flew through galaxies, stars, suns, to the native planet. He had left his father without a word. The separation from him hurt him enormously. He had chosen the flight to cool down, so that he could not feel the pain inside. During his father's thoughts he was reverberating.

"Do not do anything before I come

We will meet at the sandy mountain »

The Lord and Robby stared silently. They did not expect the Angel to leave so quickly.

“I know it was unprotocolary, but you have to understand it. Whatever happens is his guarantor that he will carry out his mission.”

“You got something to say to me?”

“Beware of Coudius. If the vote is not favourable at dawn, we will be the victims of an odious assault. I do not think he will have a lot to win but that will happen.”

“I know the plot. There was someone next to your son. Some extremely effective one can become a shadow. You'll know everything at the right time.”

“Then ... peace and quiet.”

“By Coudius, I'm careful, be sure of that.”

“I hope everything turn out right.”

Chapter 11

He knew what had happened between them, or rather he suspected, but he could do nothing. Anyway, there was nothing to do in this direction. He had to complete the mission. And that's it.

As he flew, he wondered if all of this had condemned his mother. Why had he chosen to be rigid, frivolous, egocentric? Maybe he was the real cause. Perhaps for another reason.

He felt somewhere within him, fanatical love, ready for any sacrifice, extreme dedication. His mother had previously chosen the sacrifice. Was it good or bad?

Only she could answer all the questions. Only she knew the truth. He had turned into a machine without feelings for others for one reason. He was the reason.

All her feelings were in his heart, hermetically sealed. His mother had left them there without worrying that the others would suffer. She had made it extremely conscious. Now bear the consequences.

*

Was everything real or was it a prey for a dream? She could feel the dense fog approaching dangerously, alerting her all senses.

She tried to run but found she could not do anything about it.

She felt as if she had been handcuffed in her own body. A heavy cold breeze and fog covered her completely.

It was like a dungeon made of pieces of eternity. She was nowhere, yet she was somewhere. There were clearly some clumsy bangs coming down from below. Deeply deep, a huge gallop came up. Huge limbs of fire were bruising up to fit into their gaps. In their throbbing light there was the boiling lava that spilled like a giant serpent on the cliffs blackened by the silvery soot that pretended to shriek in pain.

It was all so terrible that it was giving away, in a state of farewell to the fainting. Someone or something had taken that right, as if she wanted her to look all the way to the end.

Horror was on all sides. She felt the cold coming from above. She could feel the horrible heat that seemed to melt. Her eyes were coming out of their orbit. She screamed, as if she was doing it, but the scream was lost in the dense fog.

A giant screen appeared in front of him, presenting images of the past. Phenomenal. What was that? Dead. He has
already reached the great judgment. Was that the whole thing? Like religions of all kinds were different.

There was a voice in her head. "Nothing you have learned is true."

Everything was presented in detail. The defiant gaze of cheap sarcasm, her self-centered madness. All mistakes caught contour and life. They were like beings born of it. Relay, small, deformed, with shadows and gray faces. Demonic laughter, mocking, images of beings screaming for the pain of helplessness.

Flashes of fire floated so close to her that she felt them. He could feel the wounds of their wounds.

An unexpected apparition terrifies her even harder. It was Robby herself, who looked at her severely, then the Angel, her dear child, and then the others. They were all of the Goat people. They were frightened, and their hatred was only hatred. A deep, hateful hatred.

The screen grew white and the Father appeared. It was so stormy that what he had felt so far was just a play. She cried without realizing she was crying. The powers left her and fell on her knees.

"You, unworthy, are the one who set off a storm in my Universe. You are here to be judged by Me, for only I have this right. The evil in you has made you mistaken many

times. I wanted to see where your pride can go. You were taken from Little by evil, so I had to cut off parts of you, pieces from the body that had taken the Evil in possession. I did not know then that a small cell of Him remained in you. I did not think that bad cell would develop and affect your brain, heart, soul. I had to send a man to save you. You have not succumbed, and you did not want to come in the way of Light. You have triggered a storm in the heavens and on the earth. I sent you an Angel to save you. Unfortunately, your egocentrism turned your mother's love into something sick. You destroyed a love just by the desire to dominate. You wanted to be listened, adult, appreciated by all around you. Why? What have you done so great that all and all of you should obey you? What right did you impose on your crooked rules? With what right did you grant full rights to the Angel. Evil dictates you, but you did not do anything to stop it. In your madness you asked to be First on Earth. My beloved Terra. You never asked what you did to such an honour. Before the cataclysm you fought to get small titles that fed your immeasurable pride. You did not take into account for a moment that your belly was in your womb. Although the Angel was in you, you wanted to show those of your tribe what you are important. Why? I do not understand your miracles. And if I do not understand it, nobody will understand it. If I do not accept all of this, no one will accept them. Many have allowed your presence from stupidity or convenience. They were so cowardly and limited that they did not have the courage to challenge you openly. This is the lightness of the weak and small people. This has fuelled your belief that you are the best, the most capable ... False. If you felt the Light of the Angel and the man who tried to save you, you were not here now. Do you understand now?"

"Yes, Father."

"I am no longer your Father, you have lost this right. From now on I will be only Your Judge."

"I was wrong, I admit, but do not punish me so cruelly. I promise I'll make it right."

"Silence!!! You put the very balance of the universe in danger, because you wanted to control everything. You wanted to obey your feelings, feelings, way of life. Thanks to Robby you got your forgiveness. You will go into your world, but remember the exiled being, it is the last time you are suspended of the capital sentence. You will bear your second mistakes by a second and so do not do it. Do not even think that you are wrong ... You either purify yourself and you come to the Light, or Purgatory will burn your soul. I think the second option will happen sooner or later.

Those of the impure race of the rebellious do not have the power to see

the Light. You have recognized your mistakes and asked for forgiveness just, so I do not throw you into the Purgatory. You actually postponed everything ... Let's hope the planet that adopted you gave you a touch of lucidity. Go and tell everything you've lived and seen."

The giant screen disappeared, and with it the mist dissipated, releasing it. It fell from the top. Everything had ended.

*

He said goodbye to Lord Sor-in-Rob and Coudius with a simple inclination of his head.

He poured through the Portal, which, in a millionth of a second, teleported him to Terra.

The trip on Antares had ended well. The civilian project had gone well with that vote, and the convoys were taking off even on that sunny morning. They would bring the materials needed to build the first settler town. Robby had two mini-containers in which there were several tree varieties.

The Great Lord had given them before returning to Terra. The amount of oxygen had to be increased, so the vegetation

was absolutely necessary. The reconstruction of Earth had begun.

They were back on the plateau, eager to start a new stage. Unsealing the containers and launching the load to the sky. It spread in all directions over a radius of fifteen kilometres. The details were packed with cargo. It was good they knew what to expect. They were too excited to face surprises.

"We just have to wait for the conveyors, which, I hope, will land in the perimeter where we will install the beacon in two days. Until then, we still have something to do."

"What?"

"We'll go to the sandy mountain where we'll wait for the Angel."

"Yeah, I forgot."

Robby hoped that the separation from the Angel will not affect him, especially since he did not know when to revisit.

He started on the road without any hurry. Everything was arranged as he wanted. He already dreamed of the forests, the green fields, the flourishing cities, everything he had missed since leaving Terra.

He was forced into forced fire by Falixera.

His exits were extremely rare and short. Food was brought to him by special services, so he spent a lot of time in the

central library or home. The night was coming out and teleporting to various areas of the planet to stare at the stars.

Sometimes he remembered her. Lately, he was thinking more and more often of their moments. He sighted and sent his spirit to look for her among the stars.

Something was going to happen, for one night he manages to fall asleep. She had appeared in his dream, and the velvety voice he had never forgotten dripped hope into the soul full darkness and despair.

He was waiting for her to come, see her, feel the perfume and the silky blonde hair.

I'm the fairy of dreams,
You are heaven, earth and sun,
My immorality fades,
It turns me into a sweet breeze.

I am the zephyr of spring,
What have you been waiting for so many nights,
I will come from two stars,
Let us join in yesterday.

I would have wanted in other times,
Let me wait for you tonight,
Let's give you gentle sunsets,
And thrilling kisses.

He had immediately awakened and caught two falling stars. They seemed to smile as they passed.

Waiting for dawn, waiting for a miracle, but for nothing. The miracle would not come when he wished.

He knew everything was happening when it was supposed to. His inner formation did not allow him to lose hope.

Except for that evening, his dreams were, in most cases, very strange. Past, present, and future intersected chaotic, creating noise.

Many times, sleeping made him tired. He got out of bed, opened the fridge and took out a natural energizer, which he enjoyed with great pleasure. He then called the Command Centre to find the latest news.

All this was a routine carried out between two missions. But everything would change. He felt that things are going to change very soon. Something in him repeated this every hour of every day.

*

The lioness opened her eyes lightly and looked in the distance. She felt the sun heat intensely. A thread from the horror of that dream returned deeply into her. Was she in the Purgatory?

She closed his eyes and waited. Was this the moment when everything was over?

The heat continued to curl her body more intensely. She wanted to escape at any cost the handcuffs that held hands and feet.

She reopened her eyes to analyse the situation she was in. He turned her head to the right and noticed that she was somewhere on a mountain. Both her hands and her legs were caught in a sandstone.

In an attempt to escape from that grip, she tried to free her hands, but that only brought pain. Thousands of needles rattled her to the top of her head. There was no point in trying again. She did not understand how she got in that position.

In the horizon, dark clouds formed a compact mass that threatened to encompass the sky shortly.

She noticed how two metal objects rose up in the air. Exploded concomitantly. A green cloud then formed, as a signal began to widen. She felt very small objects all over her body that soon covered her. She shook her head vigorously to remove what she had covered. She was curious to understand the phenomenon. She immediately looked to her left and found amazingly a compact mass of live seeds that cut their way into the interior of the mountain.

She had seen something like that. Yes, they were intelligent seeds looking for their own source of water, and they kept themselves from a very high temperature in the ground. If the soil was soaked in time, it would immediately flow. They could withstand water for thirty days, then they went into hibernation. The genetic transformations allowed such amazing things.

She did not know where they were from, but it was interesting to know that Terra would have vegetation.

She had to go away. She did not know if she would ever come back to this planet again.

She had resigned and waited for him to see what was to follow. She soon realised that the dream she just came out of was still very present in her. She analysed every second to be able to remove it from the brain. She did not manage to do that, and she was angry at herself. It was like a virus that disturbed the whole system.

She had to calm down because the Father's warning struck her even stronger. The clouds had covered the sky. They were so black and they felt extremely heavy. For the punishment to be even greater it began to rain.

Now, those clouds whipped her up with bigger peaks that fell like a curse upon her body burned by the sun. Green lawns grew everywhere and turned into stunning trees. Small grass threads danced beside her. Multi-coloured flowers were enjoying the rain drops. All that lifeless land had suddenly changed.

The earth shuddered gently, and the rain clouds fled with a bark that had risen from nowhere.

The sun appeared as a joy of nature, and she felt relieved and floating. She was really floating. Her hands and legs were free. She got up and started descending the mountain.

She fell down but continued to remain suspended. She forced herself back with her feet on the ground but failed.

“Do not force yourself, it does not make sense, anyway you have no place to run.”

She looked for the source of the voice and discovered Robby. A little further behind were the angel and the two magicians waiting.

“I promised you that we would talk before we left.”

“Yes I remember.”

“You want to hear what I have to say? I cannot blame you if you do not want this.”

“I'm indifferent to you, anyway you hate me, and I think you're really glad you do not see me anymore.”

“You' re wrong again. And again, you talk without thinking. That's why I want you to listen to what I have to say.”

“Just say what you have to say and finish.”

“Understand woman I have nothing with you. I do not want you to think that I hate you. This feeling has long died in me, and I would love you as much as you to kill all the negative feelings that have been holding you for so long. They, the negative feelings, threw you on the edge of a precipice."

"I saw the abyss ..."

"If you do not take into account our advice, you will slip into the abyss that has no bottom. It's a startless and endless hat. Nobody and nothing can save you. In fact, saving is in you. Love is in you."

"Do not repeat these horrors indefinitely. We stood on the edge of the abyss. I know how it looks."

"You know what you did not understand? We exist because we are born of love to give birth to another love. We are all a sublime cycle of sensations, feelings, simple exacerbations of the known and unknown universe. We are
moments of energy floating on white nights that we are pleased to have ephemeral existence."

"Interesting, very interesting. Finally, something strange is happening. After all this, you've been able to capture all my attention."

"Your interest will increase when you find out that we are some hearts flying in ether to unite in a magic of words whispered one evening when the melancholy sunset unleashes the infinite sidereal touch.''

"Are you sweet or green wormwood?
Can you alway again my sweet torment?
Going to see never before,
You're curing my soul-pains."

The Lioness's eyes filled with tears, flowing on her face and burning with the sun. The proud woman who had cast off her love fell into a sea of despair.

"We cannot translate into any language, that touch of lips, touch that triggers a whole epic called love. Love does not know boundaries, love does not have space-time barriers because we are just simple emanations of light. The Creator has given us the power to fly in thousands of primes, which

pours as a balm over our souls lit by the fulminant desire of total fusion."

"Kill me, I cannot stand it. I do not feel angry, I'm begging you."

"Do not bother. They give you the right to life. You killed love, and I asked Father the right to wake up what you despised. You have not understood that there is a great deal of love and incantation that resembles the end of a moment of immortality."

"I did not understand, I did not mean to understand. Now it's too late."

"Offf, you're a phenomenal stubbornness. Even though the Father has caused all these to hurt you, you continue to feed them with your own life. Do not you really feel how the lip of the abyss dips easily but surely underneath you? Do not you really want to come back to normal and taste everything I've told you? Did not you want to be in glory? Turn the time, do what you want with him, make him look like a second tune or a millennium. Become one with the drops of ambrosia and nectar, then make a simple mortal and say to the dawn that encompasses you:

"I was a goddess for a moment because of love."”

The lioness rumbled, and her hands cracked over her face. Robby took her hands and shook them.

“Crazy woman, do you think what you're doing is helping something? Find peace, accept what you are, accept your destiny, repair the mistakes you have made, and speed up your deliverance. If you do not do this you will become a memory. If you do not care about yourself, think about your child. He will accompany you and take care of you. He will be your teacher, mentor, guide your steps to the Light, or assist you in your passing. You choose...”

Chapter 12

One by one, dozens of Antarian transporters came out of the hyperspace at the entrance area of the Milky Way. These conveyors were state-of-the-art and were designed to be fully self-contained for two years.

The storage and docking capacity was impressive. T-type conveyors could support two to five units of combat aircraft. They were fitted with frontal shields made of biokevlar, which could support the fire power of four S-class cruisers. But they had an glitch, a heel of Achilles. Guns became inefficient for small and medium-sized ships. This aspect was offset by the assault units they had at their disposal.

Antharian engineers were no longer in pride, especially since this type of ship had already won the prize in four galaxies. The purchase demand was rising so that these conveyors were superb. The fifty conveyors were accompanied, as they were naturally, by security ships, now famous cruisers. At the exit of hyperspace the eight cruisers released their mobile units, now occupying defensive positions.

Commander-in-command Coudius received the commanders' reports. He knew the reports of the other cruise
commanders would come, so he transferred everything on his second channel.

Coudius did not like space hunts. They were extremely infuriated and boastful. In the narrow circles he frequented, he was known to be extremely envious and malicious, and he did not deny this for a moment. On the contrary, he said that these two defects were his only capital sins. It does not stand for someone to be better.

Shortly after leaving hyperspace, Coudius, received a special report from the Supreme Council.

"I want you to bring all the commanders in here as soon as possible."

"I understand.

In the discussions with the subordinates he did not allow any interruptions or objections, however pertinent they were. He had the crazy courage to take all the risks, regardless of the consequences. Rely more on flair and intuition than on rigorous calculations.

The commanders occupied their seats in the Admiral's Central Hall. When the aide informed him that everyone was present Coudius left the command panel and turned to them.

"Gentlemen, I make you known that we are in the Fourth alert state. According to official reports, the purification foreseen in the Martian sector has failed. A large number of rebel ships have broken the blockade. Send all drones to research. I want every particle checked. At the slightest suspicion, combat ships will come into action without delay. To the gentlemen, I hope you will not forget that any mistake is fatal and is paid for. We have a long way to go to Terra. How was it possible for this Council to treat such a delicate matter so superficially? Sending only thirty middle-class ships without rapid attack support is pure madness. In forty seconds you lose ten ships, and another ten will suffer serious damage. Everything is estimated as if a supernova exploded. That incompetent commander reports that it would be about one hundred and fifty rebel ships. An where damn are hired of nobody find they?! Oh my, for this this event, the purification of Mars is suspended until new orders, but fifteen elite units arrived from the constellation Belerofon. Aha! Now let's see what happens if you stay there for so long."

The second came in and stood upright.

"Why is delaying with the permission to enter?"

"Bureaucratic things, but ..."

"Just got in touch with who's responsible for this."

"You have a connection, sir."

Coudius shrugged his voice and interrogated the Border Command.

"I'm Lord Commandant Coudius of Antares, and I think you know where I am."

"Of course, I know the purpose of your visit, but..."

"Visit that could become a permanent residence. Officially, I am also the Governor of Terra."

"The procedures for comparing customs declarations have not been completed. I hope that in the shortest time ..."

"Sir, you do not understand that we have terms to respect. Immediately turn off the passageway, set up a corridor, and in case of non-compliance, you know where to find us. Just get in touch with the Supreme Council and solve the problem at once."

"The Galactic Protocol forbids this. I recommend..."

"I do not need your recommendation, sir."

"Then there is only one way to calm you down. Use of force."

"Are you threatening me? Do not you really know who you're talking to? I could just blow up your orbital station."

"It was just a conversation. I usually do my threats. I can eject you into hyperspace immediately. My ion guns are already armed. As for a possible answer, take your thoughts with you. I have a state-of-the-art defensive system."

"Decline your identity and rank, sir, you have offended me enough."

"When you are superior to me, I will do this, Lord Commander. Until then ... goodbye."

*

Slightly undecided, the Lioness, she stepped beside the Angel. She felt like she was climbing on an escalator, wearing it lazily toward an unknown destination. Would he live in an underground land destined for the exiles or a mining planet?

She looked up to contemplate for the last time at the clear sky that left a reddish sun to shine in the coolness of a sunset. She was letting go of this last sight before she was surrendered to the unknown. The pain of separation from her planet screamed in her like a demon escaped from the inferno. A yellowish, light-coloured light passed through her eyes.

It was so passive that it resembled a dying man who, though he still has to live for a few seconds, is surrendering to the dead ahead of time.

Was this partition just a station that unconsciously cast it into an amalgam of great questions? All that's possible.

Everything seemed inert and this tardy inertia was drowned by its metallic breath, which seemed to come from the past. On the right, a dark and cold tunnel opened, ready to swallow at all times. To the left was the Angel, this good child who had accepted and forgiven all the mistakes. Is it worth his forgiveness?

She was feeling more and more of the coolness of that. He knew there was the shelter of the sad souls. He seemed to see them standing in wait, waiting for the sins or deliverance.

She wanted to be there, and she did not know what she wanted. Was she defeated? Did the eternal darkness defeat the Light of Beginning? Sequences of her life began to flourish. Could that all sort of struggle be called life? The simple answer penetrated his slowness, and the shell of exacerbated egocentrism exploded in thousands of pieces.

"Life is a universal second, and your soul is unique. It's your fingerprint. It cannot be falsified by anyone and nothing. She pursues you in future lives and pursues you beyond, in death."

Suddenly, the darkness caught her, and instantly she realized that the sordid and cold station was actually the prelude to a second consumed. A strange phenomenon enveloped her. Lyrics, an orderly order that expressed intense emotions. An unprecedented desire pushed her to become aware of them, to enjoy them.

Wild and cruel kiss agony,
You cut me off strips and yell,
In the horizon of the pitch, I see eternity,
It's raining with fire over me, innocent.

Whips deviate cruelly over the fate,
Punches hit me in ignorance, I give up,
Knives thrust stronger in the hearts,
The divine escapes from all that is mad.

I cannot die, the moment has not come,
I float between the worlds and feel that I vomit,
I struggle to beg for mercy,
But nobody hears a hoarse voice.

He looked at the frenzied light slots and wondered when this journey would end.

He still refuses to believe the mystical dogmas, apocalyptic courts populated by killer archangels who kill you with their cold eyes, not before they throw you in Tartar.

And yet the truth was somewhere out there, in the dark. His father had shown the Purgatory.

Now he felt floating in a nothingness that had no beginning or end. That was how death was supposed to be. And again, that orderly order appeared out of the blue.

It was supposed that these phrases written by someone would be the answer to her questions. Maybe it was supposed to happen. Breathe deeply and merge into them ...

I feel how death comes from the mist,
It smiles terribly, it wants me in the dark,
My head hurts, it's full of colds,
I'm trying to escape, I do not have time.

It slowly fled the blood,
I breathe jerkily, clinging to a thread,
My gaze dies, I'm no longer in me,
The desert kills one last zephyr.
The storm passes through impetuos dreams,
It change happiness into an little infinite,
Hours weep in an old watch,
Far is praying a darkened sexton.

So that was the way of non-existence. This passage that was as ugly as gods and mortals, and yet no one could touch it, suppress it.

She wanted to feel the feeling of death intensely. She was not afraid of anything. It could have been a spasmodic explosion of Eu in the eternal time of two universal seconds ...

"Mom, wake up, I'm in your ancestral home."

"Why not yours?"

"Unfortunately they will never be mine. I am from the Angels world."

*

"Sir, we've gone well with the planetary cloud of the galaxy. There were no losses in any sector."

"Do I understand that the vacuum expansion valves have created the corridor necessary for the passage?"

"Yes. It's an exceptional innovation."

"Sir, I did not ask for your opinion, make sure that all the systems, both offensive and defensive, are operational and in full alert. I have a feeling about going through the Great Asteroid Belt."

"I'll send the drones, and the hunting ships will create a passageway."

"Yes, I know, you will repeat the procedure. Only half of the ships are shipped, the others will be defensive, and some of the cruisers. You determine the number of ships that will participate in this operation. You will also take a course to intercept the planet Mars. The people in Belerofon have got there and are waiting for us. Forward to all commanders the navigation plan. I hope in no more than forty-eight hours to get close to the planet. Then we pass to Terra."

"I understand."

"How long to the Belt?"

"Up to four hours."

"Perfect, work then."

Ignoring all aerospace technology, Coudius calculated the navigation trajectory, wishing to find a comfortable corridor.

Although the devices specialized in such measurements had travelled, with a 0.007 micron error, on the central navigation map, they did not take them into account. He disconnected the central screen.

The security system announces the anomaly for thirty seconds, then all the components recovered into the secondary network. Coudius was getting nervous.

He was thinking intensly about the great escape from Mars. Where could a hundred and fifty ships disappear without a trace. It was not possible. Unfortunately, there was only one place to hide. Cold fires crossed him all over the body. Would the Great Belt be the perfect shelter for rebel ships? The probability of this theory being true was extremely high.

Could this civilization mission turn into a disaster? If an ordinary man was in command, he would have stopped the navigation at this moment and send a signal to the nearest inhabited planet to support him.

Unfortunately, Coudius was by no means a rational man, being overwhelmed by an immense vanity. Pride did not allow him to seek help even if the danger was immediate.

"Second, right away to me !"

The situation was critical, and Coudius hoped that the luck that had always accompanied him would not leave him now.

"Yes, sir."

"Retract all the ships in the immediate perimeter immediately!"

"I understand."

"Only drone units are in front. The corridor will be almost near, even if it lasts. How much is up to the Belt?"

"Two hours."

"Report the situation every thirty minutes."

He passed his hands through his hair, trying to calm down as quickly as possible. It was necessary for the mind to be as clear as possible to avoid unpleasant situations. Activate the channel directly with the second.

"Activate thermal systems. Everything needs to be prepared."

"The first unit is less than five minutes from the Belt."

"Enable and place the entire band in the fan. Hunting ships focus their attention on the outside. At the first dubious sign, fire."

The tension was increasing and the first asteroid expulsion maneuvers found Coudius walking with his hands behind his back through the command room. Opened communication channel:

"Report."

"No sign. Everything is done according to the established protocol."

"I understand, the surveillance continues."

The quiet before the storm. He felt physically, but whatever the situation was, a sense of honesty prevented him from playing with people's nerves. He was too much and felt a bit guilty. It was not supposed to be in the wolf's mouth without their consent. But where did these precepts come from which they had not yet taken into account? Curiously, they tried it all at once. Compassion, fear, guilt ... Ha ha, ha, he was starting to get old.

Perhaps he had to withdraw from work. Who knows, maybe after building the first city on Earth ....

How long and how long he had gone to the exit of the Belt. Before the communication channel was activated, the alarm sounded.

"Report !!!"

"Drone destroyed in the F-1 sector."

"Grade alarm 0. All prepared systems."

"Sir, the information has arrived. At least a hundred middle-class ships are in front of us to less than ten miners."

"Battleship; Fire! Clean the area, I want to have visibility. Two units of hunting ships by left-right hood."

Recovers the main screen and initiates the procedure that ordered it. The entire theater of operations appeared in 3D.

Rebel ships, taken by surprise initially avoidance maneuvers in the back.

Curious maneuver, especially since they did not engage in combat. It was clearly a surprise for them.

"Lower the speed and secure with two units each flank. Two crucibles in front, the rest in the back."

They advanced cautiously, changing the route as often as possible. He did not want to be a safe target.

"How long before we get out of the belt."

"About twenty minutes, sir."

"In five minutes, all cruisers will advance with sustained fire while the rest of the convoy will initiate left-hand avoidance maneuvers."

"How? Sir, repeat ..."

"I do not repeat anything. Comply !"

"But it's pure suicide."

"Execute the order or drop I you off."

It was the only procedure that could give him an advantage. On Antares the green lizard left her tail in the hands of the predators to save her life … So, the animals could be an example to follow.

"At my signal all the escort ships get out of the conveyor. Half of them will cross the cruisers and initiate attack procedures. The rest will take up new positions."

"I'm initiating the procedure to all the systems involved in the battle."

"Wait. Reports of ships in the flanks?"

"We lost half of them. Their fire power is superior."

"It is not possible. I did not think any rebels would defeat us. There is nothing else to do. Initiate the procedure. Now!!!"

The cruisers' guns came into action, sweeping together, enemy ships and asteroids. Hunting ships were engaged in combat. Everything turned into a hell. They were old kamikaze that transformed life and death into a unitary one.

"Masking curtains across the perimeter. Accelerate and let's get out of the Curse of the Belt once. Tell all commanders that in case of serious damage they leave the ships, not before they activate their self-destruction system."

The crash of the fight remained somewhere in the back. The last asteroid fragments floated, lazy, between them and Mars.

"We've got five more minutes and we're out, but ... battle ships in front. There are fifty middle classes."

"It's not possible! Slow down and enter the defensive formation. Get in touch with at least one cruiser to help us."

Indeed, fifty rebel ships waited beyond their belt in a battle formation. Someone was as clever as the Great Lord Coudius. They were face to face, threateningly close.

"I get a message asking to surrender."

"Nothing!!! Better destroy everything. Initiate retreat procedures behind the latest asteroids. Let's hope a cruiser will save us."

"Sir, I did not get an answer and as far as my system shows, it does not exist ..."

"Damn the system. Everything is ready?

If it is, then attack at once. Let's hope we get out of the way."

Chapter 13

"The following data is presented:

The rebels hid in the Great Belt, attacking the Antarian convoy that had to take part in the purification on Mars. Those in Belerofon have received a clear message from Coudius that they are unable to participate in the operation. Following the battle with the Mars rebels, the Antarians lost all offensive support plus two conveyors. The rest are damaged. The navigation system is largely destroyed. The date is not known when they reach Terra. Because of these undesirable events, we need to get in touch with Orion. I'm sure they will respond positively. They have also participated in civilization actions, even on Terra.

"You're sure there will be no tension between the systems."

"We will not make the mistakes of the past."

"Will we make a package of laws to understand?"

"Exactly. And even today. I have a set of laws that I will lay down."

And you will make remarks and annotations on the table.

"Perfectly agree, there would still be something. Can we resume talks with Andromeda and Perseu?"

"Obviously."

"Before moving on, I propose to take a break. Of course, you agree!"

The breaks were fine tricks to gather as much information as possible. The Four Wise Men of the Supreme Council each had their interests in a certain area of the Universe. Everybody wanted to have a big influence. Although, officially, they were in perfect communion, things were not so. Many times, the Great Wise One had to intervene to settle conflicts of interest. Each meeting was recorded and deposited in the central archives. The Protocol required that in every legislative debate disclosure of the name of the initiator of the procedure for the approval of a set of laws.

Wise men, contrary to all expectations, reunited in the Great Hall quite quickly. The Milky Way situation had to be solved urgently. The Great Wise One stands up, takes his voice and announces ceremoniously:

"I declare the debates open and ask my fellow Donemar to speak."

Wise Donemar was a tall and dry old man. Contrary to age, he had an atypical vitality. The blue eyes, were in a continuous alert. Whoever did not know concluded that he was a panicked, insecure, introverted person. Appearances cheated, and this gave him an edge in all the conversations they wore.

This time he had taken a serious mine. Looking at his colleagues, he began to exhibit his well-established plan.

"Paradoxically or I did not realize that the rebels would come in contact with the Antarctic fleet. Unfortunately, things did not go in the direction that we would have liked. Even if it seems a little bit dangerous my plan takes into account the cohabitation of several races. In previous colonisations, we went on racial crossing and the harmonization of concepts. It seems that this experiment has failed every time. Now it will be different. Or better to say, I wish it was different. If the conversations with Perseus, Andromeda, and Orion are to materialize, we will make the three races to stop the conflict. How do we do that? Based on very simple laws, which will be strictly observed. I will present you the laws, and then I will show you the places where the three races will develop. These laws cannot be respected by themselves, so there will be someone who oversees everything."

"Who did you think?"

"The Order of the Angels."

"I understand you spoke to them."

"Unofficially, yes. I initially agreed with the Status of Observers. They want to settle in the northern area. Find the Earth map in your computers. Interestingly, we will witness a second descent of the Elven people. People, as you know, have been on this planet."

"Wonderful. Everyone can participate. We have full confidence in your judgment. If this has been discussed, all we have to do is send an official request. This request will be done by you."

The Great Wisdom was the only one who had the right to question Donemar. The others checked the information and made a synthesis that presented it at the end.

"Continue brother, we are listening to you with the most interest."

"The Orion area is located on the two continents where they have lived. I mean the American continents. Those in Andromeda will sit on the Asian continent. Those in Perseus will live on both the Australian and African continents. The law package will establish the framework for collaboration in all areas of activity. There will be no crossbreeding in any way. Those caught that they have violated this law will be exiled to a mining planet. Any violation of laws will be punished with exile or extinction on a case-by-case basis. There will be no rigid systems as long as the laws are respected. Ecosystems of any kind will be honoured. For minor crimes Observers will make decisions according to the seriousness of the crime. For example, exile on mining planets. You will receive the law packages immediately to analyse and debate them. Before we establish firm contacts with the three civilizations, we will have to send the Order of Angels on Earth to organize security. Both administrative-territorial and extra-planetary defensive system. We cannot know for now whether the rebels have been completely annihilated."

"What do we do with the Antarians?"

"Yeah, I forgot about them. They will settle on the European continent."

"That I said, we will proceed to the immediate analysis. We'll get in touch with those of our Confirmed Systems."

*

The Lioness's departure had left Robby a bitter taste. He wondered how he could save the situation. No matter how he turned the problem on all sides, he found nothing to make him reproach this state of affairs.

However, according to the Principles of Laws, each individual was responsible for his actions.

Free will gave everyone the chance to choose. There is always a diffusion in which many variables are born compatible with precepts accumulated throughout life.

He was sorry for the situation of the Lioness, but there was nothing he could do about it. He had to get away from this problem before it affected him. He now had other responsibilities and other worries. Perhaps it was better that it happened. Something or someone had to admonish her strongly to see herself what is right and what is wrong.

At that moment he worried about the delay of those in Antares. He had not received any news. It was his thought of accessing the Portal. He wanted to talk to the Great Lord.

They needed information. He got in touch with the magicians and exposed his intentions and then teleported himself to the Portal area. Was it really necessary to leave or was there a possibility to establish a contact?

He searched the edges of the portal but found nothing to resemble what he wanted.

Active, however, the portal, setting the coordinates of the Antares system, closed his eyes, bringing Sor-in-Rob's image before him, and waited for the result.

At the moment it seemed to him the best solution A sublime song accompanies telepathic contact. He saw Sor-in-Rob in a spacious room with huge windows. He admired the landscape from an elegant armchair.

“Everything is happening with a purpose that escapes our understanding. I was just thinking about you.”

“I felt it. That's why I wanted to talk.”

“There's strange things here on Antares. Let me fix some details and as soon as I can come to Terra. However, a change of landscape is welcome.”

“Perfect, I expect you.”

Robby interrupted the contact, opened his eyes and looked away. Everywhere he could see trees, flowers, grass, life. Indeed, all happens with a purpose that escapes understanding.

But the Father has left us the power to know, to search, to struggle.

What people were they if they did not know and did not respect these concepts underlying Universal Harmony?

Maybe some simple machines designed to procreate? To procreate ... what? Other machines?

Many people did not realize that the light of understanding was everywhere. What prevents them from wanting to be happy, to taste the harmony of life? Why did he ask so many useless questions that they had the gift of removing them from the spiritual ascension?

Each individual had a mission to accomplish.

Long ago, he had seen in the Purgatory what meant not to respect the law, not to be in communion with all that was good.

The portal glowed and Sor-in Rob appeared smiling.

“I'm glad to see you again. It's a real pleasure to have you nearby.”

“I hope you are honest. I'm glad you came.”

“I did some tasks. The situation is cloudy since Coudius violated the protocol when he left for Terra.”

“He got away?”

“Yes, but there are only two damaged carriers. Navigation systems are compromised. It was somewhere between Mars and Terra waiting for the second convoy. He's barely able to start the signal. I think it has now been taken over. Anyway, I'm sorry for him. I have dismissed him according to the received orders. The rest does not interest me.”

“Rebels?”

“In that battle they lost most of the ships. Their remnants turned to Mars. They thought they would take the Belerofon by surprise. They wanted to break the blockade. They were surrounded and forced to surrender. Now he is on his way to Jupiter. Probably in a maximum-security prison.”

“Everything bad for good. If Coudius was not there who knows what could have happened. They could have reached the moon or why not on Terra.”

“From their accounts, it turns out they wanted to get out of the system. They had not yet established the final route. Coudius scared them. They thought they were trying to get rid of them. But well it's over. Anyway, we had to support the Supreme Council's committees. Reproaches have been going on for about three days. More serious is that Coudius' supporters go out into the street. He thinks he's a hero and they want the charges of insubordination to be withdrawn. To be brought and be given the title of Supreme Chancellor. We hope the spirits will calm down, otherwise I think we will have a small civil war. That's exactly the script you mentioned."

"I do not think that will happen. Your civilization is too advanced for that."

"The Supreme Council announced the civilizations that will participate in the Terra Reconstruction project. Andromeda, Perseu, Orion and the Angels Order as Observers. A series of laws have been issued that are designed to give complete harmony between civilizations. If you are interested in details about this project ..."

"Where you civilized?"

"Here on the European continent. Like that's what you say."

"Yes. It's fine and I hope that convoy will come as soon as possible."

"Let's say in five days they'll land."

"Coudius?"

"I think there is no point in discussing this issue. I hope he will die of old age carelessly."

"I hope the same thing."

"Perfect, then you have to make your host offices as good as possible. Keep in touch."

Robby took his friend. He led him to the Portal.

"May the Light guide your steps wherever you go."

"Same to you."

Chapter 14

Drift was total. No one knew where it was or what the direction they were going. Operational systems were partially destroyed. Biosystems were partially compromised. Everything was shrouded in smoke, and chaos completely reigned.

Contortioned beasts, broken walls, blood stains, people wounded in agony cried out loudly for the desire to live. Unfortunately, nothing could be done for them. Medical drugs were ineffective in such situations.

Coudius was lying on a chair in the immediate vicinity of the command desk. A rudimentary band spread, across the arm. Blood stains indicated that the brave commander had several wounds on his arm. She stared with her eyes, smiling with a sardonic smile. Does he realize that everything is compromised? Possible..

The only thing he wanted was to go back to Antares. There he was really safe. He had to consolidate his position no matter if what had happened now would have created some rumours. His supporters knew and could fix the situation. Had it been in a more populated area, it would have been great.

As far as you could see, only stellar dust was the absolute master. They tried to connect with the outside but the systems were damaged. It was an indescribable chaos on his ship. The most beautiful and performance ship, created and decorated in accordance with his wishes, was now a clinical death. A state of lethargy has taken hold of his injured limbs. More precisely a painful numbness that slowly and surely spread all over the body. They are not scared, they do not panic, they simply instigate them. Had the autoflagging developed from adrenaline?

He, the great Coudius, was appeasing in this painful leeward in the hope that everything could turn into a miracle or even know a way of deliverance by death.

Yeah, he wanted to die. This grandiose humiliation could not stand. Better would have died then in that desperate attack he had begun. He seemed to see slowly every laser beam that the frontal shields were reluctantly rejecting, shaking the ship closer to the rebels' ships. He could already see the destructive impact.

Some silly-dominated fools who would not have believed that He had no courage to destroy any obstacle. The phenomenal temperatures caused by the explosion of the ships with which it had come into direct contact had destroyed all the miointegrate systems that were in direct correlation with the ventilation systems.

The second fire dam was fatal when the deflectors shrank. They knew he could avoid a new impact, but the conveyors were still uncovered. He did not want those rebels to get their hands on them.

After the second impact, the rebels were withdrawn. They had come to the conclusion that the antarian commander was too crazy to stay around him.

He was so tired. His eyes closed. How long had he not slept?

A milky fog enveloped him. A frozen wind drove it into a tin. It was getting hotter. Where was it? What was happening?

The mist compresses, chaining it. He felt a strong presence in his mind. A tune-in voice came from everywhere. He was in the middle of a thunderstorm. A devastating storm that struck him relentlessly on all sides.

"I have come to you with a painful mortal to figure out what you want. What do you want? What do you want? I gave you everything you wanted. But in your madness, you wanted to have more, more and more. You have not realized that in the ruthless pursuit you have made miserable innocent people. You destroyed the destinies of all those who came into contact with you. Purgatory worm is awaited. It's the last time I warn you. Your parents have been dear to me because they have walked the path of Light and preached the Law. Come back in the way of your parents. Understand that you do not have a destiny of leader. Do not expect you ever to be able to lead the Earth or any other planet.You will never reach Earth because you will go to Falixera. There you will deny the evil that has taken hold of you. That's your last way to save you from spoil. Otherwise you do not, because this is my last warning. Remember, Purgatory is waiting for you."

"Sir, do you feel good?"

Coudius lightly opened his eyes. He was on the ship at the command desk. A light on the rhythmic scintillating panel. As by miracle, the communication systems had come to life. Someone had repaired them. Tap the cutoff button and emit the signal in the ether. He turned to the man behind him. For the first time in his life, he looked at someone willingly. It was revolting what he felt, but something above him urged him to do it.

"Please identify yourself."

"Soldier Crassus Antes, the Desant company."

"I understand. What is the exact situation?"

"Sir, less than a quarter of the crew members have lived."

"All right, call all crew members."

Staying alone Coudius fell back on his thoughts. He was thinking about that strange dream. He was punished for infatuation, thirst for power. But the good things he had done over the course of his life did not count?

Something told him that these things had left the Purgatory. She had to complete a mission. He was responsible for the lives of the men who he was still leading.

"Sir, all the remaining staff await your orders."

"There is actually a request. We have to do everything possible to save us. Let's solve the problem of communications. It is vital to know where we are. As far as I can see, we have an asteroid field moving in speed. There may be a black hole in front of us."

"How did you reach that conclusion?"

"The travel speed is steadily increasing."

"Terrifying. We fall from a slaughter to be absorbed by a black hole. How many people can solve the engine problem we have?"

"Two, Johanson and Peter."

"Restore all navigation systems as soon as possible. We have to get out of this area urgently. I'm waiting for you to prove to me that you are the best. Mr. Crassus I will take you to the rank of officer, you will be my second. You'll keep me informed of everything that's going on."

It could be clearly seen that the Admiral ship was attracted to something that soon would have swallowed them. The control panel animates, becoming operational.

“Commander, I report. The ship has all the functional systems.”

“Just in time. We'll go to standard speed. Relays of the lights are affected and I do not want to have surprises.”

“I report there are two drifting drives in the area.”

“Prepare the interception systems. I hope we can pull them. For now this is number one priority.”

Coudius changes the navigation course, pointing to the two conveyors. Soon they came near them. His calls were unanswered. There was nothing to show that there was a survivor. Active biometric scanning systems. Nothing at all. Main ship data was running on the main screen.

”Tractor waves in operation. Transfer all energy to the towing module.”

“I understand. Tractor waves started.”

Coudius was relieved. Stable coordinates to Terra. and active automatic pilot. At the current speed it was possible in four or five days to reach Terra. He was happy to have escaped from that immense danger represented by the black hole. The stool is coming up from the chair. He felt the need to walk and at the same time to see with his eyes what had happened to the ship. Every fiber of his body screams of pain. It was so ending that you could no longer master the tears running on the beard. It was like a shadow on the corridors that once again were of impeccable cleanliness.

The second appeared behind him.

"Antarian battle ships were intercepted. In all likelihood, they are heading towards us."

"Perfect."

He had been scared to hear the news, but he had to go back to the command room. He hurried and sat at the desk.

Open all communication channels. The radar could see small points pointing toward him.

"Antarian convoy in difficulty on coordinates 1-4-9. I'm asking for immediate help."

"Message received. Visual contact made. We secure the perimeter in five seconds. Retrieves tractor waves. All survivors should come to the center deck to be picked up."

Coudius conforms, then announces that all members leave the posts and head for the central deck. He stared sadly as the hunting ships secured the perimeter. Paradoxically, now these hunters seemed extremely sympathetic to them. They were safe. Transfer operations were extremely fast. Shortly five soldiers entered the command room.

"Sir, I am Admiral Ahelios. I have been invested in releasing you from office indefinitely. If you want to know the charges ..."

"Uninteresting stuff."

"As you wish. You will be taken over and taken to Falixera. From there you can get in touch with the Supreme Council."

"That's what I was going to do."

"You will do it after two years of home arrest."

*

Houses of all sizes, colorful screaming. Dirty streets. Bad smells of garbage. They have the gift of provoking a state of restlessness and anxiety.

Animals of all kinds walked madly in all directions. Single-eyed dogs, yellow, tattered cats, three-eyed goats and three horns, two-tailed goats.

All these animals made strident sounds that increased the uncertainty of the Angel. In what age, what age was this land that reminded him of his childhood on Terra, before Cataclysm.

They were going to the center of that place, called Goaticus, the capital of the Goat worlds. What if the capital looked like an ordinary city?

The lioness was smiling and welcoming the three-eyed look of the houses. They were as repulsive as the appearance that only bipedism showed they were humanoid beings. At their sight, they commented loudly, without a shame. The unusual clothes that the Lioness and the Angel wore were particularly drawn.

The more they advanced, the more ridiculous the beings were becoming more hostile. The angel was more afraid of the Lioness's life than his own, so he held her arm tight. At some point, strange tremors were manifesting in the mother's arm.

He looked at her and saw the transformation. The fingers of his hands were dimly visible, covered by a rough and thin membrane. Fine skin had become rougher and changed color. It was a dark ocher with black irises.

The Lioness feels she is being watched. She stared plainly at the Angel.

"Wait a minute, I'll explain everything to you when it's time and place. Let's hurry, we're losing time.

Do not use your strength no matter what happens. You understand?:

"Who gives orders?!!!"

"It was a request, my dear."

"All right, let's go, we'll discuss it later."

Twenty feet from them a three-storey building rises. Architecture and colourfulness indicated that it belonged to a leader.

On both sides of the road appeared more individuals armed with spears and swords.

The Lioness stopped the Angel.

"Let me talk to them. Believe me it's much better."

The Lioness was moving toward the crowd that was loud.

"Who are you and what do you want?"

"I am of the Carbeh tribe, the family of the Shapel."

"Prove it."

The Lioness sat down in the dust and took a prolonged rumour that had a distinct sound.

"Yes, it is. You are. But who is he?"

"He's my son."

"He'll stay here, it's impure."

"On Father, no one will do anything to him. They are the ruling spirits that are good for nothing. Stay away or command to be killed. From one of the windows of the house there was a commanding.

"Go away, this woman is flesh of my flesh and blood in my blood."

The crowd flew scared in all directions.

"My dear, I have felt you since you entered the homeland of your ancestors."

"It's not just my ancestors, it's mine. Even if I was born and raised beyond."

"You have kept your purity, but unfortunately you have to restore the ritual. Both you and your son."

"My son is of the Angels, he is pure."

"As far as I know you had a mission beyond."

"Yes."

"And? Tell me."

"It's a lot to tell. Drink from my blood and find out what you want. I have nothing to hide."

"So be it."

"Thank you for the hospitality and the appreciation you show us."

"We are all one nation and one drop of blood. My dear granddaughter, after you are full of our goodies, please split yourself so that everyone can find out why you are here and not beyond."

"I want to get rid of this oppressive burden as soon as possible."

The leader pulled out the hanger and raised the Lioness's arm. He took a cup that he filled with the blood flowing from the wound.

He lifted the cup to his eyes, stared intensely at the red ruby, and then smelled the steam. He inspired and took a sip of all the contents of the bowl.

"Good. A perfect combination between You and Her."

The three eyes of the Leader dilated. For a few seconds the body stiffened, then a tremendous spasm began. The fainting faded and remained inert for two minutes. The Lioness did not know what to do. Something told her not to touch him, to look at everything extremely detached.

After a few minutes he opened his eyes, took a long leap and rose. He stared at the Lioness intensely, then made a long whistle. In the next moment, the air was filled with other hoarseness and similar bruises.

Outside, there could be heard the sounds, trumpets, drums that filled that unimaginable rush.

"Everyone is happy for the return of your mother. She was the missing link of the great Goat Power. This feast will last for two weeks. Please choose any room you want. I think

you're extremely excited. Your mother and I have a lot to talk about."

The angel looked at his intense mother, establishing a telepathic contact, then left the throne room.

"So, are you ready for the ritual?"

"Yes, of course I am."

"You're my only niece and the only heir."

"It's not possible."

"Oh, yes. In the Outbreak War I was seriously injured. We were close to death, but our spirits extirpated several parts of my body. The implanted chips saved me. I'm half cyborg… Then when Terra got me a little and fell into my possession, I left your parents there in the plains. You were born on Terra, but your strong spirit was here with us. You brought me valuable information. Extremely precious. I did not expect to find the map of the Worlds or universal history in you. I cannot wait for the midnight ritual."

"Why then and not now?"

"Have you forgotten the traditions?"

"No. I have not forgotten anything. Everything is in me more vivid than ever."

"If you do not want to rest sit and listen to the story of your people. I'm telling you everything, but when you lead these worlds do not forget to look at the Fire Books."

"I'm listening very carefully."

"At first, we were with each other. I was a universal person until the Father's son came from heaven. He showed us the True Way. Be proud of what you are, do not care about other breeds, love your purity seed above all. These are the most sacred precepts that have remained of Him. Blessed be his name forever. In us was the Seed of the Conquerors. It was asleep, but the God of the Neon, as she was known, awakened us. And then it became the father of Billy Goat. And then, at midnight, we got up to fight with Him. Destroyers, Cruel, Unforgiving. Systems were falling one after the other. Planets the same. I was going through everything through the purifying fire. Until I arrived on Terra ... There I took part in the most gruesome fight I've ever had. That's where I felt the end, when we saw the dreamer in the dream. I wanted to kill him, but nothing could touch him. I could not even get to him. The one you accompanied yourself with was the tragedy that destroyed Everything. A lot of angels and elves have appeared everywhere. We fought for life and death without rest, without worrying about wounds, losses. But when the one who subjected Death and Life grabbed God's Nothigness, I realized there was nothing left to do. Later we had to teach, not before conditioning this. Father of the World has decided to be exiled from nowhere.

Our ships have been destroyed. It's been five hundred years since, and it feels like it was yesterday. We have never given up on our dream, so we have built underground armament factories, interplanetary bridges, defensive shields and state-of-the-art ships. Tomorrow you will see them all. We all ought to believe that we are merciful. Every year humanitarian convoys come, and clandestine trade is prolific, so we have nothing to worry about. This fierce people love me. They worship me because I know how to lead them. There is no mercy or other similar precepts. The law is clear! You're wrong, you pay! You must above all respect your customs. Thus no one will invoke the Fourteenth Law."

"How does that law sound?"

"When a leader mistakes another clan member can challenge him to life and death. This eliminates two weaknesses.Tyranny and nausea. Never give up the opportunity to invoke this law."

"Has anyone ever provoked you?"

"Yes, five times. Now let's go."

"I'm going to take my son."

"Come with me. He will come later."

The Lioness closed her eyes and inspired deeply, sending her son a great deal of peace with the urge. Everything is fine. Do not use the Force.

"How's your dear niece?"

"So much happened in such a short time."

"I understand you, everything will be fine. To go them, in the night with the full moon. Don't wait."

He went out in the cool of the night. The crowds danced, sang and drank a hint of dark honey.

"Do not be afraid, brothers and sisters are celebrating."

"You told me that again. But what do I drink?"

"Come on. I liked Terra so much that when I left I took seeds, shoots, habits and way of life."

"Is it far from the place of the ritual?"

"No. Soon we will reach the Wonderland Plain. Meanwhile, admire their joy. They're so happy you're back. You are their master."

A smooth slope descended with a reddish moon. The plain opened before them. Dozens of camp fires were lit all over, forming a huge circle in the centre. When they entered the plains thousands of acclamations met them.

"Now you're going to talk to the Wisdom Advice. Enter the Circle of Immortals and clean yourself."

"So I will."

The Lioness entered the circle of twelve pillars and shuddered as she noticed that twelve bee-eaters were stitching together. She looked closer and realized that they were humanoid beings.

In the middle of the circle, seven elderly people were seated with white beards coming down to the ground. The three horns they wore with pride were immense, bent, ready to drop. They looked at her.

"Are you a Carbeh of the Shapes?"

"Yes. I'm the last of my family."

"Do you want to purify yourself?"

"Yes, I do. I want this more than anything else."

"Who's above you?"

"The Father's Goat."

"Will you respect the laws of this world and the traditions?"

"More than life."

"Who was our teacher?"

"The god of Nothingness."

"Say sacred precepts in one sentence !!!"

"The courage and pride of what will be the keys to success and knowledge."

The last elder stood up and signalled the poles. Twelve armed men appeared behind the pillars. This split the churches, then take a horn from the girdle and fill it with blood.

"Drink from the blood of the purest and pass through the fire. Turn your spirit into Purity of the Infinite, the Immortals followers."

In front came the angel that was tightly bound by two men. It hurt her enormously that her son witnessed such ghastly scenes. She would've done anything to spare him from this torment.

She had to end this madness as quickly as possible, even if the abortions of this ritual turned her stomach inside out. She sipped all the horns and wiped the blood flowing over her chin. She felt the thrill of how the whole body confounded her. Her arms, her head and her legs were growing louder. The skin grew thicker. It turned into a platoon. Her head was the worst. Her mind was clear. Everything was spinning extremely fast. The three horns came out of her throat. Mad cravings ended its full transformation.

"You're one with us now. Go through the fire."

The lioness was absent from the horror circle. It was like a trance to the huge fire that was fed with dried bits of those sordid beings.

She passed by the Angel, surrounded the huge fire twice as if she wanted to swallow it, and then she stepped into it as though it were just an innocent walk. Her beautiful curly hair began to burn, and her horns became incandescent. When she left the fire, you could no longer know the Lioness of the past. His eyes shone wildly, and his body became a black plank.

He looked up at the moon. The strong and black arms waved up with a wild whine. After a moment of silence, the madness rallied more fiercely than ever.

"Silence! I said, silence!"

The whole assembly stopped to the contrary.

"She's my niece and she's the only heir to the throne of the Goat Worlds. We will purify our Son as the Father of the Father to remove the curse of impurity from us. Take it and purify it !!!"

"Never!"

The Lioness turned to the Leader. His eyes were shimmering.

"Purification can only be done voluntarily. As far as I can see, you want to force an innocent defenseless man to do something."

"You're right, niece. The joy of review has darkened my judgment. Let's ask your son if he wants to be one of us. Or maybe he wants to die. Son of the greatest ruler, do you want to be purified and be one of us?"

"Noooo, never! Better die than transform me. I am the Angel of the Angels, the Child of Light and the unique proponent of Universal Harmony."

"That's enough!!! Crucify the impure! Let the Father Go to receive this sacrifice of blood."

The Lioness thundered so loudly at those who held the Angel were back. She headed for the Council of the Elders and screamed.

"I invoke now and here in the name of the Fourth Father's Law!!!"

"What is the reason?"

"The use of force in purification."

"Right. So be it! Prepare for battle and the most valiant to reign."

Chapter 15

White wings come from the Light,
Flowing immortality from thousands of colors,
I feel sweet, divine,
Angels pretend to be peony.

"Nicolas. The angels are coming. Do you feel?"

"Yes, I feel them, is Robby ..."

"Time's up ... you hear."

Time came, love to appear,
The goddess from the mountains is now among the clouds,
It re-establishes through tears the feeling,
The sun petals, new flowers are born

"She came, finally came."

"Where will Angels land?"

The evening was smooth, and in the distance a cross placed on the top of a mountain lit the sky.

"We got to get there ..."

"Patience, we will arrive when Time arrives."

The full moon, surrounded by white clouds, sparkle light forests, hills, mountains.

The magicians stepped on the greasy and soft grass, listening to the spell of the leaves. It was so quiet that it seemed to them an impatience to open a subject of discussion. In front of them there was a glittering glitter of multi-coloured flowers. They approached cautiously, for they were observing a silhouette that seemed to meditate. The batons were awoken to life, but in the next second, they were quenched as if hypnotized.

"Come on, do not be afraid, I was expecting you."

"Robby? We thought that ..."

"Silence, listen to the coming."

All three of them closed their eyes, and their spirits took their flight to the high sky. The moon vibrated slightly, as if moved. The air vibrated, the trees vibrated.

Without telling him, Robby, grabbed the magi of his hands and teleported. Everything was hard for a second, and he awoke at the foot of the mountain that towered up to the sky. The trees and the vegetation formed a hail of a green, which had glittered silver.

They were waiting for the coming of the Angels as a deliverance. It was as if a burden broke from their souls and went somewhere infinitely. They did not even know when the first rays of the sun hit their faces so hotly.

Three silver ships appeared in the sky. How trained their eyes were, they could not look directly. Like a signal, all three ships were opened. The teleportation happened instantly. In front of them appeared five contingents of ... It was not possible ... Elves.

The Elves people returned to Earth. Angels came from heaven. White, with white wings, having silver peaks.

Three angels had separated from the first wave. They were heading for the great cross. Robby felt the look of the elves on them. He looked down at them and smiled.

"You have come back, you, the richest and most virtuous of the First."

“Well, I found you the Great Prelate and Protector of the Holy Land. We also welcome the Masters.”

“We're all three Protectors.”

“We know. We are honoured that I finally met you. I am Robomir of the planet Tepelus. Supreme Commander of the Elven People. For so long. We'll wait for the other commanders to come. Unfortunately, the mission in the Goat Worlds ...One of us came from there and asked for immediate help. It seems that there has been a change of leader. She's a queen. It looks like there will be some major changes.”

“My son was there. She was wandering in exile.”

“The Lioness of the Goat family?”

“Exactly.”

“Your son came from there and I think his mother took the lead. It seems like a revolt of the whole system is about to break out. I sent Ten Contingents there, and they'll leave tomorrow. I brought them here because here they will come back when it's over.

There will be elves and two cohorts of angels on Earth. However, alert is general in all systems.

“I hope it's okay.”

"Will come out."

"I'm glad you'll take the lead of this wonderful planet ...."

"Wrong, you'll stay here with us. The time has come for the one who flies through spaces and times to find the peace he has been looking for hundreds of years. I know you'd like to be with us in the front line, but it's possible. You're more important here than there."

Robby left his forehead and a sigh escaped without permission.

"The Elves people have chosen this territory to maintain peace and harmony. Do you have anything against it?"

"No, by the way, we are glad that this holy ground can be the house of the most virtuous of the First."

"You forget that you were among the First? Or do not you remember?"

"I remember everything, as if it were yesterday."

The multitude of the angels descended gently and searched the area. Some of them stayed in the air, others mingled among the elves. Both angels and elves knew Robby. It was a true legend in all corners of the universe. He was the one who had defeated the Evil, who had fooled Death.

They knew that Fate and Destiny were obeying him because he was the only one who made the stones weep, and the law of nature was one with him. He was the father of the Angel, and ... they knew of Him. It was the most beautiful love story.

As a sign, angels and elves sat in the formation, leaving a lane that placed Robby and the two magicians in the middle.

Robby felt something he had not felt before. He was shaking his soul just like that magical night. He felt her. She was not, she did not think she would meet her again. He said it was an illusion caused by the coming of the First.

A silver mist descended with them. Flower petals, rose petals ...

Where? How? How could it be that rain rose from the sky with rose petals? Even he could not do such a miracle.

The magic wands rose in the air and drew together two hearts.

A blast of rainbows enters the magic. Everything was full of the harmony he had felt at the beginning.

He had felt it when the sky had flourished with so much love and great snowflakes. He heard the lyrics flowing over all the breath:

"You gave me a spring,
You gave birth to love not spelled,
You killed a heavy burden,
My fairy of other dreams".

The answer came immediately from the mist at the base of the mountain. It was tremendous. Robby could not help himself. The tears were whistling in the face of the one who had roamed the universe in search of his great love.

You are the salvation that you smile to me
You appeared when it was foggy,
Sublime divine eyes,
They fascinated me and they gave me life.

Your candour flowed in waves,
Over a deserted soul,
You wandered across the slopes
A silence came from the sunrise.

You are pure harmony,
You are my sight with clear sky,
The pain no longer resurrects,
For it has joined us in divine.

Robby felt the whole thing spin around him, his eyes frowning, and he fell on his knees. It was too much, too much. All the hope, suffering, torment had come out of the secrets of the soul and invaded him.

"Get up from the First People. The time has come for your deliverance. I'm Marcriel and he's Telemahos. We are the Commanders."

A blond, passionate creature emerged from the fog.

It seemed floating, as if confused with the zephyrs that were enveloping it. It was her. Crissy.

The long-awaited love.

"Yes, she is the half that completes your harmony. She's yours."

Crissy raises Robby and kisses his eyes for the tears of regain. They were both very happy about the reunion.

"Yes, I'm yours forever I love you."

"And I'll love you for ever, no matter what happens."

The sun sent its wreath of crown to honour the purest love in the universe. Everything smelled of celebration, of happiness.

Everything had been done as it was written in the book of Time.Terra resurrected like a Pheonix bird.And her Protectors had to watch for the Law and Harmony never to be disturbed.

End of Volume 2

Contents

www.ingramcontent.com/pod-product-compliance
Lightning Source LLC
Chambersburg PA
CBHW070627310726
48982CB00001B/192
9780359568994